Fatma Qandil is [illegible] translator, and was born in 1958. She is associate p[illegible] (emerita) in the Department of Arabic at Helwan University in Cairo and deputy editor-in-chief of *Fusul*, a magazine of literary criticism. She has published numerous collections of poetry, works of literary criticism, and translations into Arabic, and her nonfiction has been translated into many languages worldwide. *Empty Cages* is her first novel. She currently lives in Cairo, Egypt.

Adam Talib is associate professor in the Department of Arab and Islamic Civilizations at the American University in Cairo, co-editor of the journal *Middle Eastern Literatures*, and a scholar of classical Arabic poetry. His translation with Katharine Halls of Raja Alem's *The Dove's Necklace* was awarded the Sheikh Hamad Award. He is also the translator of Khairy Shalaby's *The Hashish Waiter* (Hoopoe, 2018) and Mekkawi Said's *Cairo Swan Song* (Hoopoe, 2019).

Empty Cages

Fatma Qandil

Translated by
Adam Talib

First published in 2025 by
Hoopoe
113 Sharia Kasr el Aini, Cairo, Egypt
420 Lexington Avenue, Suite 1644, New York, NY 10170
www.hoopoefiction.com

Hoopoe is an imprint of The American University in Cairo Press
www.aucpress.com

ISBN 978 1 649 03320 8

Library of Congress Cataloging-in-Publication Data applied for

1 2 3 4 5 29 28 27 26 25

Designed by Adam el-Sehemy

The Chocolate Tin has Rusted, I'm Sorry to Say

1

IT'S BEEN WRAPPED IN A plastic bag and buried in a drawer ever since I brought it here from the old house along with all my other so-called valuables. The tin is crammed full of old poems—in blue, red, and green ballpoint on thick glossy paper—that I'd written when I was twelve or thirteen and had been saving so that I'd have something to laugh at when I got very old. Every time I opened the tin, the words seemed fainter, but the paper remained thick and glossy all over, except for the grooves left by the pen. It didn't make much difference. Those poems—or what was left of them—hadn't made me laugh in a very long time. For many years, they brought a smile to my face, but over time, I stopped caring. I wasn't planning to re-read my childhood poems; they could fade away for all I cared. With the distance of age, childhood appears strange and tiresome, a constant reminder of how much time has passed.

I have no idea why I felt like getting the tin out tonight. The old plastic bag that I kept it in was looking dirty and scuffed, so I got rid of it and picked out a new one. There were some old papers and photographs in there that I wanted to take a closer look at, but I wasn't in the mood for it just then, so I set them aside. It was then that I realized the tin no longer closed flush. The rim was bent so the two pins that held the lid in place at the back weren't lining up. They were so far from the notches they were meant to slot into that no matter how hard I squeezed the rim, I couldn't get it to shut. Every adjustment I made caused another part to bend out of shape. After I finally managed to get the tin half shut, I took the two pins out for safekeeping, fully intending to get them fixed one day.

The tin lay there on the table in front of me. I don't think I'd ever looked at it very closely before tonight.

2

"Cadbury's Milk Tray Chocolates" ran elegantly from one corner to the other in an embossed purple band. The rest of the tin was decorated with illustrations of the various types of chocolates that it had once contained, and in the bottom right-hand corner, it read:

1 lb. net
including foils
454 grammes
٤٥٤ غرام

It struck me as funny that Cadbury's was so precise that they'd gone to the trouble of noting how much the foil wrappers weighed, but had decided that Arabic readers didn't need to know that information. The tin must have come from abroad—probably Beirut, seeing that they'd spelled the word "gram" with a *gh-*. I examined the tin for other clues, but the silvery bottom had rusted.

3

There was something beautiful about the variety of chocolates decorating the lid. Rectangular, round, smooth, lumpy—bits of pistachio was my guess. The colors had faded a bit, but the brown was chocolatey enough that they still seemed real. I must have been sad when I ate the last one because it wasn't a very big tin to begin with. I like to picture myself curled up with the tin and my cat Meesho under a heavy blanket in the little sleeping nook in our living room on a winter night. That was where I slept when I was very young, before I had a bedroom of my own. I'd probably eaten most of it by myself. Meesho wasn't a fan of chocolate, and I can only assume that my father, mother, and two older brothers each took one chocolate and left me the rest. They used to let me have all the treats when I was that age. Even today, the tin overflows with joy, and I assume that's why we kept it for all those years. It might even outlast me.

4

I was never going to repair the tin. Never going to get those pins back into their little slots so that the lid would shut as snugly as it once had. It would be like stifling it. Every time I tried, I worried that if I actually did get it to shut, I'd never be able to open it again. I'll leave it as it is—half-shut; I'll just be careful not to let everything fall out.

I tried to remember how it got here, but I couldn't. So it goes. My memory is full of holes, but it's not for fixing either. The tin had been a gift—that's for certain—but not one of the gifts that people brought when they came to visit my mother during her final bout of illness. For one, it looked expensive and it felt like a part of my childhood. The fact that we'd kept the tin indicated as much. Kept the tin as in kept it empty, I mean. Unlike all the other chocolate tins in the house, Mama hadn't stuffed this one with spools of colored thread, thimbles, needles stabbed through black card and tinfoil. Nor had I stored her dentures in it. I'd kept them of course, wrapped up in a plastic bag along with a pair of her glasses with one arm missing. Nor had I used it to store any of the other things I'd inherited from her, like a lock of my grandmother Fatma's hair. Fatma, the namesake whom I never got to meet.

5

The joy inside the tin wasn't the only reason we'd held on to it. Think of how often joy disappears without a trace. Pride had to have played a part as well. I can still remember the moment the flashy car turned down our street and all the neighbors came out to gawk at it and at the two young, expensively perfumed women who got out. My father sat with the women, legs crossed, laughing, dressed in pajamas and a thick terry robe that I continued to wear for years after his death as though it had been my own undisputed inheritance. It's one of the few times I can remember my father laughing. I think the visit took place in 1969 and that was when the imported tin of chocolates entered the house. The young women laughed along with him and patted him affectionately.

I don't remember my mother being there, but she was hardly the jealous type. My father liked to brag about his Saudi students who came to visit him when he was unwell. I can't be entirely sure whether they'd been his students at the Lycée—his post-retirement teaching job—or if he'd given them private lessons, which was uncommon and expensive back in those days.

It must have been them who brought us the chocolates. The joyful tin, glamorous visitors, neighbors watching from balconies—these were all reasons to feel special. Special in the way that only an eleven-year-old girl can feel, and even now as a woman in her sixties, she still remembers the murky living room lit only by the light filtering in from the kitchen, her head buried under a blanket, feasting on chocolate, cuddling her cat, Meesho, grabbing him whenever he tried to escape.

6

A long time ago—a long, long time ago—Ramzi woke me up in the middle of the night. He was carrying something wrapped up in a tattered sheet, and I could tell from the look on his face that it wasn't a tin of chocolates. "Wake up. We have to go bury Meesho," he said through tears.

Meesho had been very ill in the days before his death. He'd been bitten by a snake while roaming in the desert around our house, and the treatment had failed to cure him. Ramzi dug a grave in the back garden directly under the window of the bedroom where we'd each take turns living in the years to come, and then, together, he and I laid Meesho's heavy body down and covered it with soil. Standing before a wooden grave-marker bearing the name of our cat, we recited the opening chapter of the Quran with utmost solemnity. A few days later, the grave-marker flew away in the wind, but none of us bothered to go looking for it.

Years later, long after my brothers had moved out, a little poppy plant sprouted in that exact spot beneath the bedroom window. When the neighbor, a young police officer, warned my mother that we could get in trouble for growing poppies, she cut the plant down in a panic, but it came back the following year. I taunted my mother when I saw the gorgeous flowers had returned: "*Allah gives blessings to whomever he wishes without limit!*" That same morning, she poured an entire bottle of kerosene onto the plant and set it on fire. It didn't grow back after that. As with anything, if you stab it in the heart, it's done for.

7

But was the plant dead? It lived on in the funny story that I told all my friends, especially my stoner friends. Later, many years after I stopped telling that story—after my mother's death, to be precise—I had to deal with her bandage and the galabiyya she'd been wearing when she died, both of which were just lying in the bathtub. The bandage was the last thing left of her, so one morning I summoned the courage to bury it outside where the poppy had sprouted and where we'd buried Meesho. As if that spot in the garden had been designated a grave back when I was a child. As I carried the bandage with the care and dignity I felt it deserved, I saw some little white things moving on it, and then when I looked closer, I realized that they were maggots feeding on what remained of my mother's flesh. It felt like I'd been electrocuted. I screamed hysterically for a while, but eventually managed to collect myself enough to dig a hole. I threw the bandage inside and quickly covered it up with soil before reciting the opening chapter, this time on my own.

8

It was pride, for sure. That was what I summoned up that afternoon. The pride of a young girl whose math teachers used to slip her the assignments they found difficult so that she would get her father to take a look. "Don't they know how to solve this?" he'd ask. "They're always bragging that their teachers graduated at the top of the class!" When she returned to school the following morning with the answers in hand, she did feel proud, but it wasn't because her father was clever. It was because she was in on the secret.

"Do you know that drunk guy over there?"
"No."
"He's saying your name."
"I don't know him."

He'd just gotten off the metro and was staggering around the station completely sloshed. Through his slurred speech, it was perfectly obvious that he was calling my name, but I just ignored him and started walking more quickly. I've lived with that moment my entire life. All these years later, I still can't erase the memory or pretend it never happened. Not even as I pour another beer, as I try to piece together what drove my father, as I observe myself, hammered, throwing up my insides. A lifetime of shame in a split-second. It lives within me, nestled too deep to ever vomit up.

9

What if I'd shaken off my girlfriends and circled back to find him? He'd have been loitering in front of the metro station, drunk as a skunk in the middle of the afternoon. What if I'd confronted him? Simply looked him in the eye with all the contempt and anger I could muster. Of course, that's not what happened. I let him get away with it, and at home the following day, he got to pretend as if everything was normal. When he went out front to water the plants dressed in his underwear—a tank-top tucked into boxer shorts that went down to his knees—where all the neighbors could see him, I let Mama have it. "Didn't he promise that he'd stop going outside in his underwear? Why can't he at least wear pajamas? I'm sick of this. I wish he would just die!"

Should I have called for the nurse to change my mother's pants every few minutes? After all, it was a private hospital. Instead, I sat my mother on a wheelchair and peeled her pants off. I pulled her nightgown up to her waist and took the basin away when it had filled with urine. "Don't worry, Mama, I'm going to clean everything myself. Don't be embarrassed." Urine soaked the floor and the smell of glucose permeated the air, but it was just us, and I had the mop in hand as soon as there was any mess. When the nurse eventually returned hours later to take my mother's temperature and close out her shift, she didn't notice a thing. Not the polished floor, not the clean patient dressed in dry pants and a clean, fresh-smelling nightgown. Everything was in its place: my mother in bed, wheelchair against the wall, basin clean and at the ready. She didn't even notice the exhausted woman who stood up to greet her when she came in.

10

"The garden died with your father," Mama used to say, and she wasn't wrong. He had looked after it dutifully even though it was little more than a small rectangular bed with a few plants that climbed against the abutting wall; the garden at the back was much larger. After he died, the scent of jasmine faded and the garden dried out to a patch of dirt before becoming an ashtray. At first, the guests who sat beside me on the balcony were too sheepish to throw their cigarette butts outside, so I was on my own, but little by little the pile grew into a heap.

Because I'd more or less given up sitting on the balcony after my mother died, it came as a shock to discover one morning that someone had stored a bunch of empty chicken cages in our garden. There were dozens of them, made out of palm stalks, piled on top of one another, covering every inch of ground between the two walls. When I saw the cages, I lost it. It felt like it was open season on our house, as if no one lived there anymore. For days, I tried to catch sight of the culprit, but I failed, and whenever I took a nap or turned my back, even more cages would appear. On many nights, I had to restrain myself from setting the cages on fire—I probably would have burned the whole house down. Then one night I decided that I would hide the cages on the roof. Rage provided the energy I needed to lug all those cages up to the roof by myself, a handful at a time. I covered them with an old sheet, doing everything I could to antagonize whoever it was they belonged to. I was worn out, but I felt a surge of euphoria and smug satisfaction whenever I pictured the shocked look on their face when they discovered that all their cages had suddenly disappeared. It was daybreak by the time I finally went to bed, so I didn't wake up until evening the next day, and when I finally roused myself and creeped up the short staircase leading to the roof, I saw that all the cages had been removed. No one tried to store anything in my garden again after that.

11

My brother came straight from the airport to the hospital where Mama was being treated. I took a deep breath as I watched him walk up the hill to the hospital, but there was hardly any need for it; his visit ended up being much shorter than we'd originally discussed over the phone. He wouldn't be able to stay for long—two days at most, he said. During the day, he'd stay at my mother's side at the hospital, and I would take the night shift. So after he arrived, I went back home, took a hot shower, and got into bed. The bed felt unfamiliar, but the scent of my favorite pillow lulled me to sleep. The phone rang a couple of hours later.

"When are you coming back?"

"Didn't you say you'd stay with her for the rest of the day?"

"Yes, I will, of course, but come as early as you can."

I wasn't able to fall back asleep after that because I was worried that something had happened to my mother. I got out of bed in a panic, dressed quickly, and grabbed my overnight bag. When I got to the hospital, I was relieved to find my mother in her room, smiling and serene. My brother informed me that his wife had called to tell him that their young daughter had come down with a nasty cold, so he had no choice but to cut his trip short. He seemed agitated and desperate to escape. He told me that he was going to spend the night at his wife's parents' house and that he'd stop by the hospital the following morning on his way to the airport. At that point, the nurse walked in and smiled at him with exaggerated courtesy, but he just ignored her. To make certain she got his attention, the nurse boasted cheerfully that she was taking excellent care of his mother, but when he glared at her, she fell silent and slipped out of the room. As he was leaving, he slipped her a bill, which she accepted with a chastened look. "At your service, Doctor."

Later, after he'd left, I was escorting Mama to the bathroom when she fell, so I called for the nurse. She ran in and lifted her off the floor, but when I tried to help, she snapped at me: "This is my job! Call me if you need to move her." When I slipped her a bill, she smiled. "Alright, then. For Mama's sake. Call me if you need anything."

12

It terrifies me that people are going to read this. Terrifying doesn't even capture it, and it's making it impossible for me to carry on. In the past, the reader would perch on my desk as I wrote, and I could reach out to them.

Now all I want to do is push them off the edge. I don't want anyone to read this. I don't want anyone spying on my life. Fine, that's a lie: writers do need readers. Someone has to share the turmoil inside me. This is suicide, I tell myself. No, it isn't. I want to scrape away the scab so that the wound can heal in the fresh air, and if it won't, the blood can just ooze out under my watchful eye as I dab at it with a damp cotton ball.

My closest friends encourage me to keep writing, but today I told my colleagues—who teach literary criticism and write commercial novels—that I was writing my memoirs, and they were dismissive. "Oh, no, no, no. Please don't be reckless," said one. The other, a novelist, suggested that I write it in the third person. His little gem of wisdom kept me laughing the entire day. Third person, are you kidding? In Arabic, we call that the "absent" pronoun, but all I want is to be present—present for the first time in my life. I dream of uninterrupted presence. I want to scrutinize every pulse of light that shines inside me until I've blotted them all out like Medusa. I want to create idols out of all my memories, then smash them to bits and sweep up the dust. I could end up an idol myself—it won't matter.

Third person? Seriously?

13

I'm thinking about buying a new tray. The plastic one that I've got is too small—one of the plates is always hanging perilously off the edge—and the hideous roses, which I failed to notice because I bought it in a hurry, have faded a bit, so it always looks dirty no matter how often I clean it. It's just a cheap tray so I shouldn't care, but I can get another one for the price of two packs of cigarettes or a few beers. It's not going to bankrupt me. I just want a tray that looks new, if only for a month.

I didn't buy the tray because I live alone. I know lots of people who live on their own who eat their meals on a little folding table that they wipe down once a day. Sometimes they set it with a little vase of flowers, bottles of ketchup and mustard, and salt-and-pepper shakers. I don't bother with that. It isn't something we did in the house growing up. For us, there was no ceremony in putting a meal on a tray and carrying it off to eat alone. Ramzi ate in his bedroom while listening to music or reading a book. Our mother ate off it when she got back after a tiring day at work or she took food on it to Ragi, who was always alone in his bedroom. Our father used to set the tray beside him in bed where he'd tune into all the different international broadcasts on his handheld radio, while simultaneously reading a detective novel. My mother had told him he could drink at home "to avoid any more scandals," so he kept a bottle of brandy on the nightstand.

It wasn't that our schedules were out of sync. We were all home at the same time, and we'd often pass the tray around after we'd used it. The only person who ever objected was Ragi, who—despite always keeping to himself or perhaps because he always kept to himself—would insist that we eat at the table together when he was experiencing one of his "fits of enthusiasm," as we used to say. "For once, I'd like to feel like I'm actually part of a family!" But he could never learn to restrain his tyrannical impulses. He informed us when the meal would be served, and he took it upon himself to set the table. We weren't to be late, not even by a minute. We teased him and acted out famous lines from the film *Zizi's Family*, in which Fuad el-Mohandes plays the buffoonish eldest brother, but eventually we acquiesced—except for my father, of course. We sat at the table, humoring Ragi and giggling among ourselves, devouring our meals as quickly as possible so that we could escape. We weren't able to sustain that family ritual more than once a month, but we did it to please him and to get him to stop pestering us. As soon as the meal was over, life reverted to the way it had always been. One by one, we returned to the tray that hung on a nail beside the kitchen sink.

14

"I can't keep covering your expenses for the rest of my life, Ragi. You're a grown man. I'm not going to keep giving you money."

Ragi was standing in front of the mirror, buttoning his shirt and tucking it into his trousers. "And I'm never going to forgive you for talking to me like that, Dad."

That must have been in the late sixties. I don't know why—I've never known why—that short, painful exchange still sticks in my memory. It's always at the back of my mind, as though it were the august opening of *The Iliad* or something. It had become legend. Destined never to fade or be forgotten. I was only eleven then, but they were both adults, my father and my eldest brother. Fate had wanted me to witness a crime for the ages. A crime that changed the course of history. It sent my brother to Germany and my father to his grave.

15

In the meanwhile, Mama rented a room for Ragi in a building that was still under construction a few blocks away from our apartment. We all lied to my father and said that he'd gone to Assiut to study math at the teachers college there. Ragi had finally managed to pass the university entrance exams after failing for five years in a row because he refused to take them. Every single year, he left the house in the morning and spent the entire day at a cafe before returning home, and it wasn't until much later at the end of the school year that my mother received the calamitous news.

When Ragi finally took the exam and got admitted to the teachers college, Dad breathed a sigh of relief. His son would end up a teacher just like him—better than him, in fact. My father ended up at the institute for middle-school teachers when he had to give up his dream of studying engineering and get a job to support his own father and siblings. He hadn't hesitated to cast his own dreams aside, so he couldn't understand why his good-for-nothing son refused to pursue a degree, which would have landed him in a higher paygrade and spared him the sacrifices that our father had had to make. He'd worked incredibly hard to become the best math teacher in all of Heliopolis despite having only a diploma and not a degree. Ragi had inherited my father's dream of becoming an engineer, but that was all that it was: just a dream. He didn't want to do the work that it required. My father lugged the dream around inside of him like a heavy corpse, but to Ragi, it was feather-light. A newborn he picked out of its mother's arms and swung through the air while my world-weary father looked on.

16

As adventures go, taking food to Ragi in the afternoons while still dressed in my school uniform and avoiding, as Mama had insisted, any of the streets that my father might take on his way back home was a fun one. I had money in my pocket—most of which I had to hand over to Ragi, but I still got my share: compensation for the perilous journey and my silence. Plus Ragi always met me at the door with a big smile. He'd dropped out of the teachers college in Assiut and decided to take the university entrance exams again—for the sixth time! Nothing could get in the way of his dream of becoming an engineer. Sometimes he let me play on the unfinished staircase on the condition that I was extremely careful not to fall. On my way home, I'd stop at the little cigarette kiosk to visit my friends, the doorman's kids, and give them a break so that they could rest or play—I don't remember which. Their father used to compliment me on my attentive customer service because I treated everyone with respect, even the construction workers who only ever bought one or two loose cigarettes at a time. I was always extra nice because I wanted to prove that I was a good little merchant like my ancestors. The shoppers were always sincere in their thanks, and when I handed the money over to the doorman, he'd say that I was good for business and that I should stop by every day. By the time I got home after accomplishing all my errands, I was walking on air.

17

"I might kill myself. I mean it. You're going to wake up one morning and find me dead."

It wasn't an empty threat; I genuinely meant it. She walked beside me in silence, and while I can't remember exactly how she reacted, I do know that she asked me why. I'm certain of it because I can still remember the answer I gave. In my memory, it's all distilled and compressed. I can remember the street we were walking down. I can even remember the rock that I propelled forward with my white sneakers. "Because of Dad and Ragi, the jerk. I wish God would wipe them out. Both of them."

You paid a price for saying that, didn't you, Fatma? For confessing your sincere wish. You meant it. You wanted them to die. You were speaking from the deepest part of your soul, and why should it make any difference that you were only twelve at the time? We pay for our murderous words, no matter how young we are when we voice them, even if we're too young to understand the meaning of death. We know that death is always hiding somewhere, waiting to steal the words out of our mouths. They're death's precious gems, its secret treasure. Using our sharp-edged words, death carries out our orders, snatching the souls of those we wish would die.

18

I'd made the threat, but I wasn't the one who went missing. It was my mother. When I came back from school, something about the house seemed strange, and my mother wasn't there to greet me as usual. Ragi was in his bedroom with the door shut, and he wasn't shouting orders at us for a change. When Dad came home early from work, I could tell he was agitated, but he was also being warm and affectionate, which was out of character. It fell to Ramzi to take me aside and explain what was happening. Mama had gone to stay with Tante Sharifa because she wasn't feeling well. I couldn't believe that my mother had gone to Tante Sharifa's house by herself—she knew how much I loved going there.

"When is she coming back?"

"In a couple of days," Ramzi said before tickling me like he always did. I giggled hysterically as I slipped out of his grasp. "Can you guess what I'm going to make you for lunch? Eggs with basterma!"

Ramzi knew how much I loved the smell of basterma sizzling in butter. A few days earlier, I'd been at the grocers with my mother, and when she said we couldn't get any, I actually started to cry. That was how much I loved it. "I don't have enough to get it now, but I promise I'll get you some as soon as we get paid." As I gazed at the basterma twisting in the air above the chiller, its aroma wafting, I got hunger pangs, and—although I was old enough to know better than to beg or throw a tantrum—I couldn't stop my eyes from welling up. I stepped away so she could finish shopping and engage in her monthly conversation with the man behind the counter about how bad the subsidized rice continued to get. I didn't want her to see me cry. To this day, a whole lifetime later, whenever I long for something—even a body—I see a basterma dangling before my eyes and its scent wafts over me.

19

I was standing in the kitchen watching Ramzi prepare the meal that I was so looking forward to when Dad came in, smiled, and stood beside me, patting me on the head as if I were a kitten.

Mama didn't come home for the next five days, or perhaps longer, but no one explained to me the nature of the dangerous illness that caused her to stay away so long. No one made me eggs with basterma again after that first morning, but Ramzi did compliment me on my good behavior. My father had raised my allowance slightly because of the circumstances, so I used the money he gave me to buy ful midammis from the cart near our house, which catered primarily to construction workers. Normally, my mother handled all the household spending, which was probably why I was too embarrassed to ask for eggs with basterma again. I decided to stick to ful instead.

One morning, my father took me to Tante Sharifa's house to visit my mother, who was lying on a narrow bed, looking gaunt. She hugged me, and I guess she must have been crying because it makes me cry now just recalling that moment.

My mother didn't come back with us as I'd anticipated she would, and my father and I didn't go straight home after we left either. He and I stopped at Abu Shanab, the juice bar in Triomphe Square that I used to love. I got to sit at a little metal table right out on the street and drink a big glass of sugar-cane juice one tiny sip of joy after another until the whole thing disappeared; my father drank beer from a bottle in silence.

20

Several days passed before my mother—unsteady on her feet and constantly dozing—returned home and visitors whom we rarely saw started turning up. Every few days, Mama's sister would appear with other relatives in tow, including an elegantly dressed and imposing man whom my mother called "Uncle." My mother and I would occasionally visit him at his very grand apartment in Korba, but the only thing that I can remember about it now is the massive covered balcony. It was big enough that they kept a bike out there, which the children, myself included, were allowed to ride.

From snippets of conversation about the importance of reconciling and all the back and forth that that precipitated, I gleaned a vague sense of what had happened, but eventually I heard the story from start to finish. I can't recall exactly when, but I'm pretty sure it wasn't long after. My mother had gone to see her brother, who was entertaining guests at the time, and when she leaned over and whispered to him that she needed to borrow some money, his wife stood up and shouted at her in front of everyone. "Enough already! Leave him alone. He isn't made of money. Shame on you!" The color drained from my mother's face, and she bolted to the door. My uncle tried to catch up with her, but his wife fainted at the exact same time, supposedly, so he had to run back to her side, and my mother let herself out.

21

Things I'm certain of:
My mother wandered the streets.

She swallowed a load of sleeping pills in order to end her life.

As she wandered, unable to wrap her mind around the humiliation she'd faced, she was hit by a car.

The driver wasn't going very fast, so she only suffered some bruises and scrapes. My father was summoned to the hospital, but she refused to go back home with him because she didn't want us to see her like that. Rather, she didn't want me to see her like that. She told him to take her to her best friend Sharifa's house, where she could mend.

22

For years, they didn't speak. Finally, as my mother was preparing to go on pilgrimage, she took the initiative. She came home one day, looking irritated, and told me that she'd gone to my uncle's house, where his wife had greeted her warmly and hugged her. I was an adult by then—nearly thirty—so I wasn't very pleased by my mother's sudden forgiveness and received the news begrudgingly. Later, when my uncle paid us a visit at home, I received him begrudgingly as well. He'd aged, but he was still very stylish with his Kent cigarettes and gold Dupont lighter, and he boasted to us about his daughters, who were working at prestigious hotels. I'd dropped out of university and moved back home after my divorce, so he offered to help me get a job at one of the hotels. "But, Uncle, I'm a poet," I said, declining the offer with pointed snobbery.

I knew he thought I was a loser and claiming to be a poet was not the way to persuade him otherwise. He gave me a paternal look, which I think was sincere, and asked, "What do you mean, you're a poet, my dear? You have to get a real job so you can help your mother out at least." My old dislike of him had returned with force, so I simply walked out of the room in silence.

After he left, I confronted my mother: "I never want to see that puffed-up jerk here again. Bragging about his chambermaid daughters!"

"He didn't mean anything by it, love."

"You can forgive him if you want. He's your brother. But I'm never going to forgive him, and I'm never going to love him. I don't want to see him here ever again."

I couldn't control my anger, so I went into my bedroom and started breaking things. My uncle had managed to hit me where it hurt the most. I knew I was a failure—all I'd managed to do was publish a few poems in magazines—and that I was sponging off Mama's meager pension, which I had no right to do. I spent it all on cigarettes anyway. Still, I couldn't get over the impertinence of that stranger coming to our house for the first time after years of bitter estrangement and trying to play the role of the caring uncle, which he'd never once been.

I knew, even though I would never admit it to myself, that my cousins weren't actually maids. They worked as receptionists in Cairo's fanciest hotels while they were finishing their degrees—earning their own money, wearing nice clothes, and helping out with household finances. Meanwhile, all I did was sit beside my mother and write poems, consoling myself with the belief that they would never know the joy of writing. My mother and I both used to get so happy when we saw one of my poems in print. They would never know that feeling. But I had doubts. Deep down. I didn't know if my journey had begun or what. I couldn't even imagine what my journey was supposed to look like.

When Mama knocked, I let her in and she just wrapped her arms around me and let me bawl my eyes out until I finally calmed down. That was the last time I ever saw my uncle because he died a week later. My mother asked me to go with her to pay our condolences, so I softened my stance. Perhaps to atone for my rage. When I entered my uncle's house for the first time in many years, his wife welcomed me with a hug. "My dear, you're all grown up!" I distracted myself by examining all my uncle's fine possessions. Mama may have been grieving, but I still managed to make her laugh on the way back home.

"That woman cannot be stopped. She was all dolled up for her husband's funeral! I bet she'll have a replacement by tomorrow! Did you see their house? I can't believe he got all that money just from scams. Please don't be upset, Mama, but that brother of yours reminds me of Stephan Rosti. He even trimmed his moustache to look like him!" She agreed wholeheartedly, and I guess the old wound finally healed that evening.

23

It had been a very deep wound. Mama had two brothers, but the youngest—her favorite—had ended his life for reasons that remained opaque to all. That left my dashing uncle, whom my mother and aunt entrusted with their powers of attorney so that he could manage their properties for them.

Whenever we walked through Korba, she would point them out to me. "Do you see those six shops along the arcade? They used to all be one big shop, which belonged to your grandfather. We'd be millionaires now if he and your uncle hadn't sold it to pay for their women!"

The story I'd heard was that before he got married, my uncle was a playboy, and he spent all the proceeds from the sale of the shop on "the Greek girl," as my mother used to call her. My mother and aunt forgave him after he swore that the shop he'd inherited from their father came with back-breaking debts and he didn't want people to find out that he was bankrupt. His plan was to make a new start with his reputation intact, and because he was actually bankrupt, they took him at his word. Whatever money he had left went toward getting married, and then he and his wife had one child after another.

When my mother was doing well—in those years that my father had work in Saudi Arabia—she let my uncle and his family stay in our apartment in Triomphe Square for months. "Your father was very generous. He was an angel when he wasn't drinking. He never once asked me what I spent the money on." The whole time she was in Saudi Arabia, she sent money to my uncle every month, and she even paid off the overdue rent on our apartment when we returned to Egypt, while keeping it a secret from my father. That was before things had got so bad that my mother had to borrow money from my uncle from time to time.

For years, I could hear her muttering to herself, "He kicked me out of his house! In front of all those people. He kicked me out of his house in front of all those people because of his wife. After everything I did for him!"

24

I can't remember anything about our apartment in Triomphe Square apart from the stories Mama used to tell me about my uncle and his family living there when we moved abroad. I was told that it was a beautiful and elegant apartment, so even though I've always disliked Heliopolis, I still feel a speculative longing whenever I go past Triomphe Square, which remains familiar to me somehow despite all the traffic and transformation.

The story I heard was that we moved to Saudi Arabia for a time, but all I can actually remember is that we lived in an apartment with a dark staircase that led to a storage room—or it may have been a wooden partition belonging to another apartment, I don't really know. It was a room that we were forbidden to go into—that's all there was to it. Neither the door nor the apartment featured much in my family's stories about Saudi Arabia. I climb up the staircase, up the first step, then the next, before my mother shouts at me. My memory snaps shut and sinks into darkness.

That was probably around when I was learning to walk. Memory-less. We have to learn to walk before we can make memories; otherwise we just absorb them from the stories we hear. We have to go to school, as well, because school is where memories, often painful ones, are made. Happy memories are weightless. They tend not to stick around for very long.

25

I can't remember any of the houses we lived in before we moved to Alf Maskan shortly before I turned six years old. Not even our house in Suez, where I was born when my father was working there. I think what happened is that my father went to work in Saudi Arabia shortly after I was born while we stayed behind in Suez. We only ever went to visit him there, which at least explains why I have no memories of the place. Whenever I try to remember my early childhood in Suez, which still appears on my ID card as my birthplace, the sea unfurls and the roar of waves drowns everything out, washing away any memory before it forms. I can picture the wooden cabin we lived in on the beach even though the cabins disappeared long ago.

Our neighbors were foreign technicians—Russians, Italians, and others from around the world—who came to work on the canal in the early sixties. The whole place smelled of grilled and fried fish and crabs, which my brothers used to catch in tide pools on their way home from school. I can remember them tossing a big bag of crabs at my mother and nagging her to start cooking. "What's the big rush? This one's still moving! You want me to cook them while they're still alive?"

One of our neighbors was an adorable little Swedish boy, and I remember he was with us that afternoon, playing, giggling, banging his spoon against the table like we did. "Bless you, you sweet little boy," Mama said as she watched him. She loved him, and he used to cling to her as though she were his mother. He used to run to her, crying, when his father would beat him, and she'd hide him in our cabin. "That bastard hits him with a belt buckle. Because his mother isn't here to protect him anymore. That man's a technician from Sweden, if you can believe it! He doesn't deserve a son!" I can remember my mother's lips trembling as she muttered. I felt bad for the boy, who was very beautiful, but he wasn't my friend. He was older than me. I think he was seven—around the same age as my brothers. I had only one friend, an Italian boy called Massimo. He was older than me, too, but only by a year, if that. We had a secret language that we whispered back and forth—him in pretend Arabic, me in pretend Italian—and we'd crawl underneath the cabins when we wanted to hide from the world. There, on the sand, meters from the sea, we traded kisses.

I can also remember sitting on a little chair in a huge hotel kitchen. Someone sets a mug of milky tea, some cookies, and a bag of peanuts in front of me. My mother filled in the rest of the details. "One day, you weren't feeling well, so I didn't let you go out. Or maybe I kept you at home because I thought you were bothering the staff at the casino; I can't remember. Anyway, that same afternoon, the manager and the chef both turned up to ask if you were feeling okay. They were distraught. They said that everything had been a mess that day since you hadn't showed up, so I never stopped you from going there again after that."

The story comforted me. It still does, in fact. It makes me feel that I was well-liked as a child. Well-liked and desirable. Not to the staff at the casino, none of whom I can remember at all, but certainly to Saad, whom I remember very well. Maybe what I remember best is the dirty sheets and the stale odor of the bed where he lay beside me like a silhouette. Both of us naked. His body was long and skinny, mine just four years old. I showed him my parts. I can't really remember what happened, but there was a strong smell when it was over. I didn't feel ashamed or upset. He was kind and sweet, I guess, and if he hadn't insisted that I not tell anyone—"especially not Mama," who I was not in the habit of keeping things from—nothing would have spoiled my enjoyment. But that admonishment—one he repeated after several such occurrences—made me dislike him, and when he tried to get me alone in his room to say goodbye since he'd finished his degree and was about to return to his hometown, I managed to slip out of his grasp even though he pursued me all the way to the door. I felt shrewd like a grown woman, and the memory of it makes me laugh to this day. "You got away from him with the discernment of a woman in her thirties," I tell myself. "You've always known how important it is to put an end to relationships like that."

I can still see a hand gripping mine, swinging my entire body through the air before plunging me down as the sea roars up, flooding the cabins. I feel like I'll drown in the wave before it recedes, but I catch my breath and scream, though I can't be heard over Ragi's laughter as he jumps from the wall of one cabin to the next. The waves below surge and recede. "Don't be scared, you wimp, I got you. Don't be scared."

26

I've never been a coward, and I can prove it. Two years later, my mother and I were sitting in the garden out in front of our house one evening in Alf Maskan. As I was about to start school, she made a point of warning me never to let anyone touch my body. "Mama, do you remember Saad, our neighbor in Suez?"

I told her everything that had happened as though it were perfectly ordinary. Her face went as pale as a block of ice, but that didn't scare me, nor did her trembling lips.

"That son of a bitch. I'm going to kill that son of a bitch," was all she said, over and over again.

She didn't kill him. To me, it seemed like the conversation had gone smoothly, especially after I told her about what had happened when I went to spend the night with Auntie Fatma's kids at their house in Ain Shams. My mother loved that woman. She even trusted her with her own body, stripping down naked in front of her without the slightest embarrassment so that she could sugar the hair off. In the dark of her house, Auntie Fatma used to separate me from the other children so that she could introduce me to another type of pleasure.

I'm certain that my mother was devastated that evening, but I only realized it after I got older. The poor thing had listened to her child recount horrible things while suppressing a giggle. To this day, I can't fathom how she made it through the night, but I know that I slept peacefully after sharing every last detail with her, which was what I always did. Nothing dramatic transpired in the days that followed; if it had, I would have remembered.

We never spoke about those incidents again for the rest of her life. She must have thought that I would eventually forget about them if we never talked about them again, and I certainly didn't feel like bringing them up. Not even on those days when we sat together on the balcony for hours in our house in Nozha, talking like best friends and sharing memories. Whenever I considered asking her the only question that still preoccupied me as an adult, I chickened out. Why didn't she send me to a doctor to check my hymen after what Saad did to me? I kind of assumed that she would say that she'd asked a friend—probably Tante Sharifa, the one with the best head on her shoulders—and she'd told her to pretend that nothing had happened, or else maybe she'd read in a book that hymens grow back at that age. I myself couldn't remember exactly what happened during those incidents. It was as though my memory of them had become permanently muddled after that night. When she was putting me to bed, she said, "Promise me that nothing like that will ever happen again," and I promised. "Swear by the holy book," she said, so I swore by the holy book. "Promise me you'll never keep anything from me ever again." I promised her, I swore to her, even though I had no idea what swearing by the holy book meant. At that age, I still couldn't get my head around what seemed to me like two complex and contradictory messages: "Swear to God, swear to me." Both seemed sacred—I could understand that.

The next morning, I went to school for the first time and, as my mother held my little hand in hers, I could feel something new sprout in my heart, something heavy that I'd later name "the birth of memory."

27

I always say that I was born in Suez in 1958—which is true—in a cabin on the beach, which is a slight exaggeration. I'm not lying. I just don't really remember my first few years on Earth. I don't even remember what my family said about them. It just strikes me as fitting somehow that a poet would be born by the shore.

I could have asked my mother, but unfortunately she's dead now. She died without knowing that I would grow to crave her stories, which I always pretended to find annoying. I can't ask my relatives because they're either dead or out of touch. All I have left are a few photos dated in my father's neat handwriting. Everything else was lost or destroyed.

I've never forgotten Suez and our life there, and I think that's why I want to repair my memory. I think I was born before my father went to work in Saudi Arabia, but he was only there a short time anyway—two or three years. We moved back into the same wood cabin when he returned, I think, shortly before moving back to Cairo, into a house in Alf Maskan.

We—by which I mean me and Mama because I have no memory of my brothers being there—continued to spend the summers in Suez for years after we moved back to Cairo. We would stay with her friend Umm Fuad, a warm and generous host, and her many children. Umm Fuad's house was two or three stories tall, and it was the only house my mother ever sent me to on my own. I went ahead of her because she had to wait back in Cairo for my brothers to finish their exams, but I never cried at night or felt homesick when I was there.

At bedtime, I used to squeeze myself into any unoccupied spot in the girls' bedroom, and I always fell asleep looking forward to the next day's adventures. Out of all the children, I was always the first in line for pocket money even when my mother wasn't there, and Umm Fuad was very generous to me, which made the other children jealous. Sometimes she put her eldest daughter in charge of handing out money to us children, who couldn't wait to stop at the ice cream cart on our way to the beach.

Umm Fuad's house was probably the only place where I sat on the floor, eating ful, falafel, and hot bread with other children. We made a game out of stealing delicious bites right before the other one could take it. They were the only family to send their daughters—one after the other—to come live with us in Alf Maskan while they were studying at the university despite there being two young men in the house. They weren't the least bit anxious about that, and it meant that their daughters were spared the many inconveniences of student housing.

For years, we spent the summer in Suez, but it all came to an end after the 1967 war. We moved to Nasr City, and Umm Fuad and her family joined us there as did many other displaced families. They lived on the other side of an empty desert plot that separated our house from my school, which was in Rabaa El-Adawiya

Square. My mother never stopped visiting her old friend, but Umm Fuad's children weren't as fun-loving as they'd once been. They never got excited when I invited them out to play, and eventually I stopped. Their childhood had ended when they saw their home destroyed.

28

Despite the many oaths she swore on the night of my confession, I don't think my mother did anything about Saad. Otherwise, I would have heard about it on a subsequent trip to Suez or when I was an adult. The story faded completely as though it had never happened, and because we never spoke about it again, it was my story from then on. I owned it, and I was free to tell it however I liked. I gave it life with each recitation, and it lay wrapped up in my heart like my other irreplaceable possessions.

I doubt, too, that she ever confronted Auntie Fatma about what I'd told her because she continued to come to our house in Alf Maskan and then in Nasr City after we moved . She still worked for Tante Sharifa, too. Tante Sharifa, the keeper of my mother's secrets, the wise and reasonable one. My mother did prevent me from ever going home with Auntie Fatma again. She probably made up some excuse so that she'd stop insisting that I go over for a sleepover. But that didn't stop us—me and her—from sneaking in some fun while my mother washed dishes. Hurried fun, because my mother watched us like a hawk most of the time.

Sometimes I try to remember seeing Auntie Fatma in any room other than the kitchen at our house or Tante Sharifa's house, encircled by a group of women, who were usually laughing. She would take each woman into the bedroom by turn, and when they emerged with flushed faces, arms, and legs, there would be a glimmer in their eyes. They teased one another when they came back into the kitchen, and I would giggle alongside them—even though I didn't understand the jokes—because I wanted to be included. Whenever I did, my mother would tell me off and order me to go play somewhere else. "We're having an adult conversation. Stop butting in!"

I have no memories of Auntie Fatma carrying a mop and bucket like Auntie Saadeya used to; I can't even remember her dusting anything. All I can remember is that she washed a few dishes and starred in a farce featuring women's bodies.

She was dark-skinned with a broad and tall figure, but she had no trouble squatting down between the women's thighs to remove the hair with a "gentle" hand as they often said, through grins, when they returned. Despite having to wait on one woman after another, she was always very cheerful. As happy as she'd been on those nights when we were alone together at her house.

She married countless times. Whenever she wanted a man who wanted her back, they would write a marriage contract between them, and she would invite him into her bed and her house, which she shared with her two children, Mona and Mahmoud, who always seemed completely helpless. Whenever I tried to get them to play with me, they would keep their distance because they were afraid of their mother, who often beat them with a belt—displaying real cruelty—over and over till they stopped screaming. The belt was followed by insults while the children cowered in a corner and cried.

Her marriages rarely lasted very long. My mother liked to tease her: "Aren't you sick of him yet?"

"They're all the same, Mrs. Suad."

"I guess it's almost time for the slap then." That was what usually happened. After about a month of marriage, Auntie Fatma's sexual desire would usually fizzle out, so she'd slap her husband hard across the face and tear up the marriage contract before kicking him out of the house. In his wake came a bundle of his clothes and the worst insults imaginable.

Most of the time, the battered husband would just sit on the ground in front of the house, crying and begging her to take him back, but that was life. They were finished, and she was already on the hunt for her next victim.

Auntie Fatma's clients were constantly telling stories about her. My mother, for one, never got tired of telling the story of when Auntie Fatma came with us to the beach at Ras el-Barr. She could never tell the story from beginning to end without breaking out laughing. On the morning we arrived, Auntie Fatma insisted on getting into the sea straightaway. She didn't even wait for us to unpack. She changed into a dark red swimsuit that showed off her large ebony body and that she'd bought especially for the trip. The sight of her glistening skin caught the attention of a man who decided that he would try his luck. He followed her, circling her in the water, teasing and flirting, and although she tried to brush him off several times, he wouldn't be swayed. She decided to adopt a different tactic and began to act like she was interested in him, encouraging him coquettishly to come nearer. When he got up close, she grabbed him by the penis and refused to let go. All the man could do was scream.

"Say, 'I'm a bitch.'" He did. "One more time. Louder," she said. "Say, 'I'm a bitch.'"

The man screamed. "I'm a bitch, I'm a bitch. Please let go. Please. Please let go. You're going to kill me. Please. I'm begging you."

No one rushed to help. Both the peculiarity and hilarity of the scene overshadowed the man's distress, so the people on the beach and in the sea just gawked and laughed. They didn't seem like they wanted the incongruous performance to end. When Auntie Fatma finally let the man go, he swam back to the shore with difficulty and staggered out of the water on legs that could barely hold him.

My mother used to say that men were crazy about Auntie Fatma and that she knew all the tricks of how to flirt and lure them in. She also used to say that when Auntie Fatma liked a man, she became a completely different person. She transformed into an obedient, graceful, and feminine woman, dolled up in red nightgowns. She was the picture of tenderness until she got bored, and then her other side came out. The side that we all saw. Her scandalous marriages were no secret, but people still wanted her. They wanted to see if they could outdo the men who'd come before.

She had Mona and Mahmoud when she was married to Amm Bastawi, her first and longest marriage. He was dark-skinned and so short that he didn't even come up to her shoulders; when they walked side by side, he looked like her shadow. He was a dandy, however, always dressed smartly in a clean galabiyya and crocheted skullcap, a sword slung on his right hip. He had a thin moustache and big, hazel eyes, and if it weren't for the battle scars on his face, he would have been handsome. Out of all her men, he was the only one who was allowed back home after a big argument—after storming out with his clothes in a bundle, vowing he'd never return. They made up "for the kids," she said, between marriages. The couple walked unmolested down dark streets on the way back to their house in Ain Shams from ours in Alf Maskan; not even the small gangs of nighttime thugs dared. All it took was one cold, stern look from Auntie Fatma for them to dissipate. "What are you kids up to?" She'd ask in a low, menacing tone. "Get out of here!" They valued their safety so they scattered.

They weren't scared of Amm Bastawi's sword or the pistol hidden inside Auntie Fatma's galabiyya, which no one had ever heard of her using. Rather, what scared them was her famous record of winning fights, and according to my mother, that was something that Auntie Fatma had inherited from her own mother. Her mother was a short, vicious-looking woman who had worked as a paid thug for a while and who'd spent the better part of her life as a police informant.

My mother may have been afraid of Auntie Fatma, or she may have felt that she offered her protection. Or it could have been both, and maybe that was why she never confronted her about what she'd done to me. Alternatively, she may have felt that the woman's lust had no boundaries.

As usual, I made friends with the workmen who were putting the finishing touches on our house in Alf Maskan. My father, having ascertained that the house was livable, had returned to Saudi Arabia, and it was just us. One night, one of the workmen snuck into the house, and my mother heard him opening a drawer in her bedroom, where I was sleeping beside her since my father was away. She saw the workman's face in the faint light coming in from the hallway as he grabbed whatever cash and gold jewelry he could find. He looked over at my mother, but she pretended to be asleep until he left. The next morning, she called Auntie Fatma and Amm Bastawi, who came and guarded our house for days after. She insisted that she wouldn't report the theft to the police. "What's gone is gone. I don't care." All she cared about was me. If my friend the thief had invited me to go with him, I certainly would have gone along with it. Her instincts were borne out when she caught him loitering outside the house after Auntie Fatma and Amm Bastawi had left. I had called to him enthusiastically from the window, and when she saw him, she made a gesture to convey that she wasn't going to say anything. He didn't come back again after that. Auntie Fatma and Amm Bastawi begged her to tell them his name or to describe his appearance so that they could nab him and bury him deep underground, but she refused every time. Eventually everyone forgot about the incident and my friend.

29

I was born in al-Arbaeen, which was the most famous working-class neighborhood in Suez back then. "You were my easiest birth." My mother called for the doctor, who gave her ether, and then she gave birth to me without any pain. I wasn't a troublesome newborn either. She told me that she didn't produce enough milk when I was a baby—she was nearly forty at the time, but her explanation was that she was still mourning her own mother—so people told her to give me yogurt. With impeccable hygiene, she made it herself every day in the warmth of a dim lamp before putting it in a bottle. She used to forget about me sometimes when she was cooking because I didn't cry when I got hungry. "Where's that strange noise coming from?" She'd wonder to herself before remembering and running to my bedside. "You didn't cry like other kids. When you got hungry, you'd start to coo."

I used to drink a cup of yogurt with two spoons of sugar every morning until I was well into my fifties. I'm not sure exactly when that habit stopped, but I do know that I still can't stand any form of illumination that isn't an incandescent bulb filtered through a lampshade. Perhaps it reminds me somewhere in my subconscious of the warm, shaded lamp-light that fostered the yogurt that sustained me as a newborn.

Umm Fuad and Umm El-Lul were my mother's only friends in Suez. Umm El-Lul was her favorite, and she maintained a friendship with her even after we moved out of al-Arbaeen. She always spoke of her with gratitude, as though she treasured her, even at the end. She was our neighbor—"our loyal and dependable neighbor," as my mother always said. My father liked Umm Fuad and her family, and he was kind to her daughters when they came to live with us. He always made sure that they didn't lack for anything. He liked listening to my mother's funny stories about the friends she'd visited in Suez, but whenever she mentioned Umm El-Lul, his expression would change, and they would have the same argument they always had.

"I don't understand how you can be friends with that woman?"

"She's my best friend!"

"She's a dancer! You couldn't find anyone else to befriend besides a third-rate nightclub dancer?"

"She *was* a dancer! Was. In the past! She gave all that up before we even met her. She repented and got married. Are you going to continue judging her even after she repented? Who do you think you are? God? Even God welcomes repentance!" That was where the conversation always ended, my father in a huff and my mother continuing to visit her friend whenever she went to Suez.

My mother knew the real reason that my father didn't care for Umm El-Lul, but she never confronted him about it. Around the same time that my mother met her new neighbor, she started having doubts about my father. She told me that women used to lean out of their windows in the morning to flirt with him when he was on his way to work in a spiffy suit, bright white shirt, and tie. "Your father was so handsome and well dressed, and all their husbands wore only galabiyyas and had rough skin." Apparently, one morning, my father turned back to look at some of the women who were flirting with him, and that worried my mother, so she called her dancer neighbor over for a chat. They weren't close friends at the time, but my mother opened up to her about her fears, and Umm El-Lul assured her that she would take care of it.

A few days later, Umm El-Lul came over and told my mother, "You have nothing to worry about, Suad. Your husband isn't the flirting type. The only thing he's looking for is a drink. You can relax." I don't know how Umm El-Lul tested my father because my mother never told me, and for some inexplicable reason, I was never curious enough to ask. I guess she came onto him and he turned her down and then spent the rest of his life hiding it from my mother because he didn't want to "shock" her and resenting Umm El-Lul for it. For her part, my mother couldn't exactly confess that she'd conspired with Umm El-Lul to test his loyalty. Maybe that was what cemented their life-long friendship. It persisted even after they'd drifted apart and even after Umm El-Lul died and my mother mourned her with copious tears. They shared a secret and had been accomplices once. That makes people close.

30

Our house in Alf Maskan spanned two floors and overlooked the narrow passageway, which divided the "villas," as they were called, into two facing rows. We needed an extra bedroom for Ragi, who insisted that his be set apart from the rest of the house, so my parents carved out a beautiful and large bedroom from the living area on the ground floor, which overlooked the back garden.

Upstairs, there was a large bedroom where my parents slept and a second, smaller bedroom attached to a large balcony. The balcony had once been a bedroom with an adjoining balcony, but my father had decided to expand the balcony at the expense of the bedroom so that we could spend summer nights outside.

I probably slept in my parents' room or downstairs on one of the sofas. It didn't matter, and I couldn't have cared less at that age—I was six. Too young to know what preferences were, or to ask for my own room as the only girl—"make the boys share" was how it usually worked, at least at my girlfriends' houses.

31

Alf Maskan eventually went "downhill," as my mother frequently said. Back in the fifties, the neighborhood was lovely and new—perfect for middle-class families in search of calm surroundings because the well-known areas in Heliopolis—like Roxy, Korba, Ismailiya, and Triomphe, where we used to live—had become so hectic.

Their finances had been boosted by my father's posting to Saudi Arabia, so they went searching for a villa to buy on the outskirts of Heliopolis and settled on Alf Maskan. On each block, the villas were organized into rows, and they all looked the same, but they were "villas," and at the beginning of the sixties when we moved there, you couldn't describe them as working-class housing. They offered some privacy, but it was only notional because all the villas shared a wall and everyone could hear what was happening next door with minimal distortion.

Umm Muhammad lived next door to us with her husband, head conductor on Cairo's trams, and their children. She was good-natured, funny, and down-to-earth. She used to make my mother laugh hysterically. They became friends, but their relationship was always quite formal because for all that Umm Muhammad genuinely liked my mother, she was aware of the slight class difference that separated them. We could feel it whenever she compared her many children—especially her dark-skinned girls who had kinky hair—to me and Ramzi, who were nearly blond and had green eyes. My mother used to chide her lovingly for making such comparisons and would remind her of the principles of "good parenting." She used to reassure Umm Muhammad's daughters that "Just having dark skin made them beautiful." That said, there's no doubt that my mother was grateful for the little bit of distance that Umm Muhammad put between them by calling her "Mrs. Suad" rather than just "Mother of so-and-so."

My mother always gave her advice when she fell ill, and Umm Muhammad would do things to surprise her like taking a whole course of antibiotics in one go so that she'd recover more quickly.

We'd been living in the house for less than three years, when Mama began insisting that we had to move. It wasn't on account of Umm Muhammad and her children but because of Amm Sayyid, who lived in the villa across from ours and worked as a clerk in the office of the president. Every couple of days, we'd hear screams and curses coming from his house. Neither I nor any of the neighbors could understand why he treated his children so brutally. Whenever the shouting got bad, my mother and the other neighbors would run across the street to rescue the child he was wailing on. They'd loosen the restraints, take the belt or stick out of Amm Sayyid's hands, and push his short, stocky body away from the child, whose face he had pinned against the floor with his foot. My mother would bring the child back to our house to clean them up.

We weren't friends with Amm Sayyid's kids. They didn't play with us in the lane that separated the villas, but we'd always see them watching us from the window as if they were their father's prisoners. Even when he wasn't home, they were frightened of him. His wife was rarely seen, as well. He used to do all the shopping himself, and we rarely saw them go out together.

My mother realized she couldn't take it anymore. Even though she missed Umm Muhammad—as she often said—she had no regrets about the move to Nasr City, the next promised land for Heliopolis families, and one that was even quieter, which is what my mother was always looking for. She had other friends, of course: Auntie Sharifa and Auntie Salwa, whom she'd known for years and could be herself with. They used to call her by her first name, no titles, and they lived in the suburbs of Heliopolis in apartments, which weren't grand but were tastefully furnished.

32

I know I'm in trouble when I get lost in Cairo, especially at night. Sometimes, I take the wrong flyover and find myself on an agricultural highway or somewhere equally unfamiliar where every intersection is unfamiliar, too. I tell myself not to panic and that I'll find my way very soon either by asking someone for directions or, more recently, by relying on GPS, but when I eventually do get home, I'm exhausted, and not just because of the driving. It's all that stress. The only thing that helps is a cold beer as soon as I've walked through the door.

One night a long time ago when we were living in Alf Maskan, one of the girls from Ain Shams who'd come to help my mother with the shopping invited me to go to the market with her. I had been outside riding my bike in the lane separating the villas, and because I knew that Mama wouldn't let me go with her and because the girl promised that we'd be back before she even noticed, I didn't ask her permission.

Six years old, more or less, sitting against a low wall—I don't know where—with my bike beside me, I stopped passers-by to ask if they could tell me how to get back to Alf Maskan. Each one of them took pity on me and asked a few questions before giving up and continuing on their way. The girl had seen her mother's husband in the market, so she got scared and took off running, abandoning me. That was the excuse she gave my mother afterward when she interrogated her. I cycled down roads I didn't recognize until I got to one that seemed kind of familiar, so I took it, but when I finally got to the area with all the villas, I entered the wrong passageway. When I next stopped—in front of a villa—to catch my breath, a dog lunged at me, barking, and I scampered, leaving my bike behind. After making sure that the dog was tied up, I went back to collect my bike and pushed it along until I finally reached home.

When she saw me, my mother leapt at me just like the rabid dog had. The neighbors held her back and I did my best to dodge her curses and slipper-thwacks. "Be grateful that she's back in one piece, Suad! Thank God. Let her be. She's been through enough."

When I was older, I confronted my mother about lashing out at a child who'd been lost and traumatized. She told me that she'd walked the streets for hours looking for me, asking everyone where I'd gone and who I'd gone with, but no one knew as I'd managed to sneak away with the girl unseen. My mother said she thought she'd never see me again and it felt like her life was over.

I think that incident was one of the reasons that Mama wanted us to move. She spent the following year looking for another place to live—somewhere where she could better control her little imp.

33

We moved into an apartment on the fourth floor of a large building in Nasr City where the elevator became my favorite playground. As usual, Ragi claimed the largest room, which was the master bedroom, so my mother and father closed the dining room off with painted wooded panels to turn it into their bedroom. I slept in a curtained-off alcove next to the dining room on a pink aluminum bed, which I can still smell now as I write this. Despite the adjustment, the new apartment felt spacious. It had two living rooms, which my mother furnished with the elegant wooden set from Assiut that she'd inherited from my grandmother, a daybed upholstered in striped silk, a beautiful model sailboat in wood, a statue of Aphrodite in plaster, and some other small decorations from our old house.

Moving from Alf Maskan in Heliopolis to a completely different district of the city felt like an adventure. What really mattered was that our new apartment, like the one before it, wasn't a rental so we could maintain our middle-class position, which gave us much pride, especially since Alf Maskan "had gone downhill" as my mother often said toward the end of our time there.

Between our new ten-story building and my school, which was named after Abd El-Aziz Gawish, lay a wide street and open desert. In the other direction, two identical buildings stood behind ours in a line on Khedr El-Touny Street.

The new apartment had a big balcony, which I liked, and I liked my new school. The tearful goodbyes with friends as we left our old house had faded from memory, and I didn't think about them at all when I was walking to school through the desert, dressed in a stiff khaki pinafore, as my chubby classmate Khaled led the way, singing, "O Adawiya" and we echoed in chorus "A-hey, a-hey, a-hey!"

My new school was much nicer than Nabil El-Waqqad Elementary in Alf Maskan, but I did miss the sky-blue pinafore that we used to wear. The teachers at Nabil El-Waqqad had been strict and violent, so I had done my best to avoid punishment by getting good grades, but there was nothing I could do about the cane on my cold hands when I was late for roll call in the mornings. I can remember blowing on them to warm them up so the cane would hurt less. There wasn't much corporal punishment at Abd El-Aziz Gawish school, and what little there was, my mother eventually saved me from. One morning, I refused to go to school because I was already late, so she came with me and laid into the teacher who was standing by the gate with a cane. He never hit me again after that.

After school, we kids would gather in the street outside our building and play, the girls playing blind man's bluff and the boys marbles. I liked playing marbles, and after I showed the other kids the marble collection that Ramzi had assembled for me with his exquisite taste, they enthusiastically invited me to join them.

We used to play war, too. Our building took turns being Egypt or Israel, and when we played as Egypt, we used to chant, "We're going to fight the Israeli chickens!" The low brick wall in front of the building provided cover as we attacked the enemy. The team playing Israel was destined to lose every time and have their soldiers taken prisoner, but we always distributed the weapons equally. We made rifles out of pieces of wood, putting a nail on one end and a clothespin on the other. We'd stretch a rubber band from the nail to the clothespin and load it up with a paper projectile so that it would shoot through the air when you released the clothespin.

The only thing that upset me was that all the other kids had bicycles and I didn't. I would watch them race around on their bikes, and they'd occasionally let me go for a spin. The small bike that my father had brought back from Saudi Arabia for me when I was three had a training wheel, so it was essentially a tricycle, and it was far too small for me. My mother had gifted it to one of Umm Muhammad's sons during our move and promised me that she'd buy me one that suited my growing frame.

No matter how much I sobbed and wailed, my mother couldn't afford to get me a bike. Every month, she promised to, and every month, she let me down. There was just never enough left over after she'd given my brothers their allowance and paid for their tutors. One summer month, she was able to set aside enough from the household budget in order to get me the next best thing: a scooter.

I'd already told her how much I liked the one that one of her friends' sons had, so when she returned home one afternoon carrying a scooter wrapped in colorful paper, I bolted to my feet and cheered and then kissed my mother over and over and over. Of course, it wasn't as good as a bike, but scooters weren't very common in those days, so I finally had some leverage with the other kids: "I'll let you ride on my scooter, if you let me ride your bike."

I liked an older boy called Ala, but I kept that information to myself, and one evening, I discovered that he liked an older girl, who was also called Ala. I sat on the staircase outside our building, my scooter lying beside me, and cried as I watched them together. He grabbed her shoulder and they smiled at each other. Then he kissed her furtively on the cheek before they set off together on their bikes, which appeared to move as one. I was nine years old and in the third grade when a girl told me that her brother liked me and that it made him jealous to see me playing marbles with the other boys.

Her brother was a humorless sixth-grader called Mahmoud and unsurprisingly his unspoken affection failed to make up for the heartbreak caused by the gregarious and handsome Ala.

In spite of the war, we had three happy years interspersed with fun holidays, including ones that came by surprise, like the day of Egypt's defeat in the 1967 war. Ragi was taking the university entrance exams for the first time, and Ramzi was in the first year of secondary school. My father spent hours at home, which was unheard of, sitting on the balcony from time to time with a mug of warm cinnamon milk or anise tea. My mother cooked meals and occasionally surprised us with a simple cake.

In joyful moments, my father would give me a bath or tickle my feet, and the house would fill with laughter. When I think back on it now, it occurs to me that my father and Ramzi were trying to make up for the toys that I used to get when we still lived in Alf Maskan. They tickled me because they wanted to make me laugh, but also because they wanted to see me laughing. Ragi and Ramzi used to pick up a Corona chocolate bar for me when they came back from the cinema. They'd hide it under my pillow so that it was the first thing I saw when I woke up. "Who got me chocolate?" I'd scream with excitement.

It was usually Ramzi who replied. "An angel came looking for you last night, but when he saw you were sleeping, he decided to leave the chocolate under your pillow." I knew it had been them, of course, and would give them big smooches of gratitude.

Ramzi's friends, who were always over at the house, were another source of amusement. Sometimes when he went to the kitchen to make them sandwiches and cups of tea, one of them would sneak away to give me a long kiss—a new delight—and teach me to close my eyes. I always took my time before shutting my eyes because I wanted to be able to recall the entire experience again later that night when I was alone in my narrow bed exploring my body's private pleasures. My parents never noticed any movement on the other side of the curtain, but once when my father drew the curtain to check on me, I pulled my hand away quickly and he pretended not to have seen anything.

The pleasure didn't last, though. My father walked in on me and one of Ramzi's friends, who swiftly and gently pushed me away and pretended like he was bouncing me on his knee in all innocence. I could tell my father's blood was boiling, but all he did was walk out of the room. Later that night, my mother took me aside, but she wasn't interested in hearing any confessions. All she said was, "Your father wants you to know that if he ever sees you sitting on someone's lap again, you're going to get a beating." The threat was direct and unmistakable, and I understood that there would be no looking the other way next time, so I began to steer clear of Ramzi's room when he had friends over.

I never found out what happened to Ramzi's friend, but he stopped coming over after that. It wasn't until we'd moved back to Heliopolis and my father had died that he turned up at our house once more. My mother was as happy to see him as Ramzi was because his mother was one of her good friends. I was in the first year of secondary school by then, and he'd just graduated with a degree in engineering and had bought a new car, which he wanted me to see. He suggested we take it for a spin, but when he tried to kiss me, like he used to do when I was a child, I pushed him away gently and got out of the car.

Ramzi was very popular. He had green eyes and blond hair, which he used to wrap in my mother's worn-out tights for hours after washing it so that it wouldn't get poofy. He wore bell-bottoms and floral shirts, but only ever in muted colors. I never saw him in red trousers and a pink, lace top like other boys in the sixties. He was still macho, as he liked to say, despite adopting the trend of long hair and sideburns. Ragi, on the other hand, preferred the old-fashioned style, and he kept his hair short and frizzy, with long sideburns that led to a tidy beard.

The girls loved Ramzi, and they didn't mind that he was short, but that didn't stop him and Ragi from complaining to my mother constantly about her cursed genes. They also used to mock me jealously because I had taken after my father and would eventually outgrow them. "How did you end up giving birth to a tall daughter and two short sons!"

My mother couldn't stop herself from smirking, but she did her best to hide it. "But you're both so handsome! Do you expect to be perfect in every single way?"

All Ramzi had to do when he wanted to meet a girl in the street below was step out on the balcony and gesture to her, but if one of the Palestinians who'd come to study in Egypt and who lived in the building across the street dared to flirt with the same girl, a fight would break out between the two buildings. Ramzi would summon his many friends of diverse ages to back him up, and the shouting would reach all the way to our apartment.

When it was all over—after the police came, broke it up, and forced the two sides to make up and apologize to the neighbors who'd been disturbed, and after my father assured them that he'd see to disciplining Ramzi—he'd shut himself in his room and tend to his bruises. Then the following morning, he'd recount for us with excitement how he'd taken care of "the students across the street" and how one of them had actually cried as he begged Ramzi to lay off. He wanted us to know that the fight wasn't about a girl. His love of country and self-respect were at stake! "There's no way I'm going to let a Palestinian flirt with an Egyptian girl like she's easy!"

Ragi joined in the fights from time to time, especially if it seemed serious and they brought out the sticks and chains. The doormen in the neighborhood would get involved, too, at that point. Ragi wanted to protect his younger brother and that was what made my mother start to panic and have palpitations. Dripping with sweat, she'd run to the entrance of the building and push her way through the brawling men until she could reach Ragi. When Ragi got violent, it was no joke. He could grab a guy's head and bash it against the curb repeatedly in stony silence. If the others didn't prize him out of Ragi's strong grip, he'd end up dead, so my mother was terrified that he'd kill somebody one day with that silent, violent rage that he stored up. She didn't worry about Ramzi when he got into fights even if they did cause a lot of commotion. With teenage boys, the damage rarely exceeded scrapes and bruises.

34

For the third year in a row, Ragi left the house in the morning and sat in a cafe until the university entrance exams were over for the day. Then he returned home to our mother, who'd been waiting restlessly by the door. "Everything went well, and I'm gonna be an engineer!" Of course, as soon as the results were released, everyone found out that he'd failed for being a no-show. To escape criticism, which never worked anyway, he shut himself in his grand room and listened to classical music while reading something from the impressive library that he'd diligently assembled from Helmy Murad's *My Library* series and the Hilal novels. Beneath the glass topper on his massive desk, he displayed poems by Baudelaire that he'd copied out by hand and a photo of our mother's brother who'd ended his own life. "You'll always be in my heart, Uncle" was written at the bottom.

Ramzi felt quite sheepish when he caught up to his older brother in the final year of secondary school. I could hear him begging Ragi through the bedroom door: "If you don't go to the exam, I won't go either!" He was true to his word, but only for the first year. He took the exams the following year, but he didn't score high enough to be admitted to medical school like he'd dreamed. He enrolled in the Institute of Technology before it was elevated to the College of Technology, but he decided that he was going to re-take the entrance exams, and two years later, he finally got admitted to medical school.

A gloom settled over the house. I think my father started drinking again, and my mother stopped waiting by the door to make sure that I'd got out of the elevator safely. Many times when the elevator got stuck between floors, I'd give up banging on the wall and just sit on the floor in the dark by myself until someone realized I was missing. She stopped asking me to take my school pinafore off when I returned home, too. I kept it on when I went out to play and up until I went to bed. I remember another child's mother asking me, "How can your mother let you run around like this?" That was before the horrible day. I was talking to one of my friends at school when she spotted something on my shoulder and gave me a look of disgust. After she'd turned and walked away, I looked down to find a louse crawling on my pinafore and promptly squashed it. I pretended to be sick for a few days so that I wouldn't have to go back to school until the incident had been forgotten.

It had been a long time since my father had given me a bath, a long time since my mother had applied mercuric oxide to my hair before braiding it. For a long time, I'd seen her holding her head in her hands after she came out of Ragi's room, where she'd sat listening to him for hours. As soon as she'd leave, he'd call for her in a monotone, "Maamaaa, Maamaaa, Maamaaa," before she ran back to his side. For a long time, I heard the three of them—my mother, Ragi, and Ramzi—talking about depression and psychiatrists, who changed from one week to the next because they weren't making any difference.

I watched Ragi having to lean on Ramzi in order to make it to his bedroom, heard him complain about the pain of electric shocks, watched my mother cry in the kitchen by herself; everything else is a blur. Everything except the moving truck and the back of a taxi, where I sat with Meesho on my lap trying to escape as we drove to our new apartment in Nozha in Heliopolis. This time, a rental.

35

The worst thing that could happen to me after I die would be if people started repeating clichés out of this book. For my life to be a cliché. It makes me queasy to think that my life could be a lesson. I forestall that would-be hell by using language that is totally stripped down. I refuse to hide behind metaphor. The lives we lead become more salacious after we're dead, and stories are the only thing that quench the rabid thirst.

36

Our new apartment wasn't as large as the ones we'd lived in before, at least the ones I could remember. It had three bedrooms, but they came at the expense of a small, windowless living room right beside the bathroom. The balcony off the small kitchen was long and narrow as was the one that wrapped snake-like around the front room overlooking the street. That was the room that Ragi claimed, of course. The only other balcony, which was off the back bedroom, had standard dimensions and overlooked a decently sized garden at the back.

I didn't care about any of that stuff, though. I was content to play in the sandy patch at the back before my father incorporated it into his small garden. It was the first thing that I was drawn to when we got to the apartment, and I was very happy to discover that my marbles didn't roll away there like they used to on Nasr City's slippery streets.

I quickly made new friends so the ones I left back in Nasr City receded in my memory and the ones from Alf Maskan were completely erased. My parents enrolled me in a private school that belonged to one of my father's friends who'd "been blessed," but it was shameful to attend a private school back in those days so I wasn't pleased.

There was some joy in it, though: I got to take the tram to school and buy a ful sandwich from the shop on the corner on my way. And there was pain: our teacher Mr. Abdel Rafi terrorized us all. He used to put a pen between the children's fingers and then rap the back of their tiny, trembling hands with the sharp side of a ruler.

I was never punished like that—on account of my father, but also because my cousin had done well at the school and graduated to middle school, paving the way for my success, though it was hardly necessary.

Mr. Abdel Rafi's punishment-parties were painful and terrifying. My father had sworn to me that "he wouldn't dare" lay a hand on me, but, I sat at the back of the class nonetheless—unlike the rest of the high achievers—and avoided making eye contact. "It's just one year and then you'll be done," my mother said. "You'll be in middle school soon. At your dad's school, Heliopolis Middle School."

I told myself that the school year would pass quickly and that I'd soon get to go be with my friends—my father's co-workers whom I'd known for years. I still have a photo hanging up in my house today of me and my classmates in elementary school dressed in scout uniforms flanked by our teachers and the principal, all women.

I think that was around the time I told my mother I wanted to kill myself.

37

I benefited from my cousin's academic achievement in other ways, as well. My uncle, my father's brother, bought his son a new bicycle for his outstanding performance on the exams at the end of elementary school, and when my mother and I went over to congratulate him, I saw his old bicycle parked in one of the rooms. I conveyed that information to my mother in a whisper and when we went back home, we took the bicycle with us.

Despite my euphoria at finally having a bike of my own, it wasn't until we got home that I saw the poor state it was in—it was rusted and needed new tires. I left it in the garden and went to bed in tears, but when I got home the following afternoon, I received a surprise that still moves me to this day: the bicycle was inside our apartment, looking shiny and sporting new tires. My mother stood beside it, beaming. "Your father took the day off work just to get your bike fixed." I loved my father so much in that moment. His unexpected care took me by surprise, and I was so grateful. I wanted to give him a big kiss, but I was worried that he'd get annoyed and push me away like he usually did. Instead, I blew him a kiss as he stood by the front door watching me do wheelies and all the other tricks I'd longed to practice when the most I could hope for was borrowing someone else's bike for "a quick spin." He waved back at me with encouragement.

38

She was trembling when she got home, so I listened closely as she explained to Ramzi where she'd been. How one unfamiliar alleyway had led to another and then another before she eventually came face to face with a strange man and his menacing wife. A family friend had gone with her, but she was certain that she could have been murdered or raped and that no one would have ever found out. "I think they're drug dealers. They looked like it anyway. And they're loan sharks. I can't believe I went through with it, but I didn't have any choice. If he wants to go so bad, he can go. Maybe it'll do him good!"

After she'd signed all the IOUs, she gave Ragi the cash to buy a plane ticket, but when I saw him again two days later, he was dressed head to toe in new clothes and every penny had already been spent.

39

Ragi had a good-for-nothing friend who was constantly being kicked out of his parents' house, so my mother would take pity on him and let him stay with us. Not long after he moved to Germany, he sent us a photo of himself in the rug store where he worked, standing next to a "pretty Austrian girl." That was where Ragi got the idea—which soon began to plague him—of traveling to Europe like other young men his age and working at a gas station or washing dishes for a summer so that he could save up enough to buy a Peugeot to use as a taxi.

After spending all the money my mother had struggled to get together for him, he promised her that he'd buckle down and come up with a better plan. He wrote to an engineering college in Germany and enclosed his only successful entrance exam result, which had earned him admission to the teachers college in Assiut, and they accepted it.

When my father discovered that Ragi was actually living in a rented room in a building that was still under construction, fires broke out at home, but it wasn't like he could take the entrance exam for a seventh time. Ragi's hope of traveling to Europe seemed unlikely, but others had managed to pull it off. In the meantime, Ramzi had set off on his own course and started studying medicine, leaving Ragi besieged.

My mother didn't subject herself to another dangerous adventure the next time. Following Tante Sharifa's advice, she bought some electric appliances on installment, and then sold them off. She even bought the plane ticket herself because she refused to trust Ragi with the money again.

The flow was constant—photos from Paris, then Germany, postcards of museums and clean streets—while at home, we faced a crisis every time an installment came due.

My father got to open the letters before anyone else did, and from the way he'd correct my mother on certain details of Ragi's life, it felt like he'd memorized them: "Actually, in his third letter, he said that he—." The first time we heard an unfamiliar, steady ring, my father leapt to his feet. "That's a trunk call! That must be a trunk call from Germany."

We heard Ragi's grumpy voice on the other end: "Let me talk to Dad first! I want to talk to Dad first!"

"I'm here, Ragi. I'm not dead yet!" said my father, sounding equally grumpy.

I'll never forget that last exchange for as long as I live. It didn't quite blot out the memory of Ragi saying, "I'm never going to forgive you, Dad," although I could see that they'd forgiven each other. Now I know that the reason I can never forget it is because I've never forgiven either of them.

40

I was in the last year of elementary school and Ramzi was in medical school when my father, who was retired by then, suffered an angina and was told by his doctor that he needed to stop drinking. He'd begun working at the famous Lycée as a senior teacher, teaching math in English and improving his skills in other languages, as well. Since childhood, he'd had a knack for languages, including French, which got him a job offer to teach in Algeria. The position came with a good salary, which was a huge relief, because we still owed installments as part of the scheme for getting Ragi a plane ticket. The family would relive the glamor—long since faded—of the time when my father worked in Saudi Arabia.

"If your father had ever agreed to offer private lessons, we'd own whole buildings by now," my mother once said to me. Despite his talent and fame, he gave very few private lessons in the limited hours when he could keep himself sober. He only started after my mother allowed him to start drinking at home, but he always returned from his lessons empty-handed except for a few bottles, which soon joined the other empties in a crate beneath his bed.

41

They were completely separated by then. My mother slept in the large bedroom overlooking the garden at the back, and my father had his bedroom in the middle of the house. Ramzi had taken over Ragi's old bedroom, which overlooked the small garden plot. When his friends came over to study, they could just step up onto his balcony from the street rather than having to interact with us.

I think I used to sleep on the daybed that we'd inherited from my grandmother and that faced the bathroom door in our cramped living room, but I'd also sleep beside my mother on occasion. I've spent my entire life trying to remember where I slept in those years. I once joked to a friend that "If I could only remember where I went to bed at night, it would resolve all my issues."

42

The separation—the one that would never be undone—came after a loud argument, which might have been common enough in other houses.

"You're a bitch," he said.

"And you're a son of a bitch." My father then proceeded to walk into the bathroom and punch through the small window in the door.

They'd never called each other names like that in front of us before, but in the aftermath, they kept a lid on their hostility. Ramzi was closer to our father than I was, but he always refused to go ask him for money for the household expenses when my mother told him to, so I had to do it, which I really resented. One time, my father decided to let me in on a secret: "The only reason I haven't divorced your mother is because of you kids. If it weren't for you, I'd have left her a long time ago." I could have killed him, and he, seeing the contempt in my eyes, stopped there.

"Why don't you just get a divorce?" I asked my mother when I brought her the money. "We can just live with one of you, and then this whole thing will be over. It's got to be better than all this drama. He just told me that he'd 'made sacrifices' for me. Can you believe it?"

The vicious argument that precipitated their ultimate separation came when the dream job in Algeria vanished. When I asked my mother what had happened, she refused to tell me. I was an adolescent about to start high school, and the memory of my drunk father calling out to me in the street in front of my schoolfriends was still fresh in my mind, so my mother was careful not to make things worse. "He didn't pass the interview," she answered tersely. "We have bad luck." Even Ramzi, who used to tell me everything, shut himself up in his bedroom for days like Ragi used to do, and it didn't matter how much I loitered when I brought his meals to him on a tray—there was no way to get through to him.

My father had been dead for years by the time I learned the truth. When I got older, got a divorce, and suffered some setbacks, Ramzi became more open to talking to me about our father. When my reactions—my hatred even—no longer made any difference. He always began the same way: "Listen, you didn't really get to know Dad. That's why you didn't like him. I got to know him better because I'm eight years older." Ramzi explained that he'd accompanied our father to the interview himself—"I wanted to make sure he got there"—but that he refused to let Ramzi follow him inside.

"I'm your father, not your brother. Don't you forget that."

"It's just one day, Dad. Just today." My father gave Ramzi his word, but as you can probably guess, he turned up at the interview completely hammered, and the dream of Algeria disintegrated.

At First, It's All Love, Brooding, and Violins

1

WE WERE DOWN TWO AT home. Ragi had gone to Europe and Meesho was dead, so that left four of us: my parents, Ramzi, and me. I was about to start high school, having done so well on my end-of-year exams that even my hyper-critical father couldn't deny it. He had to retire his usual response: "You only got a 95? My students all get 98." I felt as though I'd failed whenever he said something like that, but later I learned that he used to boast about my scores to his colleagues.

"So you're the daughter who's distinguished herself in academics, music, and games?" They'd say when they called the house. "Don't you think you should leave something for your brothers to be good at?" It never made me happy to hear strangers repeat his praise back at me; if anything, it made me dislike him more.

Ramzi progressed through medical school somewhat ploddingly and had to re-take a few exams, but he never failed a course. He borrowed books and course notes from his classmates whenever he could, and he bought only the things he absolutely had to: a skull, bones, and the books his professors insisted that he buy if he wanted to pass. When we ate together, he and my mother would pretend to be full so that I could have more meat.

Ramzi and I started studying together on the days when his classmates didn't come over. In the winter, we'd light the primus stove in his bedroom for warmth, and in summers, we'd drench the floor. One day, Ramzi complained that I was too focused on studying, so we painted the skull together. We gave it a moustache and black-rimmed glasses, and Ramzi moved its jaw like it was a talking puppet. Laughter filled the room.

I don't know what kind of sacrifices my father was making at that point. In the old days, he used to come home with a bag of sweets or chocolates each month for Ramzi and I to share. Of course, I always finished my half in a few days, but Ramzi was more disciplined, and he took great pleasure in eating his remaining treasures in front of me for the rest of the month.

His friends were over all the time, but none of them harassed me even though I'd grown into an adolescent and drops of blood had begun appearing on my nightgowns. They listened to Sheikh Imam and The Beatles and would go to the movies, occasionally taking me along with them. After the film, we'd stroll, and they'd discuss camera angles, direction, and plot structure, which all went over my head, but I enjoyed when we'd stop for sujuk sandwiches.

One of Ramzi's friends wrote poetry, so he showed him some of the vignettes I'd written, and he told me that I'd make a good *writer* one day. I was elated and instantly developed a crush, but he turned up with a girlfriend the next time he came over, so that fizzled.

Ramzi used to invite his own girlfriend, Maha, over to the house, too. My mother and I really liked her, and she was clearly in love with Ramzi, but at one point he admitted to me that while he "admired her greatly," he wasn't in love with her. He told me that he'd been frank with her about how he felt because he refused to "lead anyone on," but despite all his frankness, she stuck with him for a long time.

Moving from middle school to secondary, I left behind the teachers and principal whom I'd known ever since I was a little kid. I can still remember the violin that they occasionally let me take home so I could practice for my recitals. Even though I only ever learned to play by ear, we still won several competitions. Our fiercest competition came from The English School, where they had a pristine and imposing stage the likes of which we'd never seen. If the music teacher hadn't inspired us not to feel like imposters, I don't think we would have won. "This is just a private school at the end of the day. Are you trying to tell me that public school girls can't beat them?"

Leaning on my acrobatic cycling experience, I learned how to do a pommel horse routine for the gymnastics team. I loved hearing my classmates and teachers gasp as I sailed through the air, and though I never managed to win a medal in any of the school competitions, I still have the old photos.

2

Things changed when I got to high school. The advanced classes I enrolled in cut me back down to size, and the mid-year exams made that painfully clear. I had to work very hard just to scrape into the class top ten.

My father had nothing to say about my sudden plunge. It didn't seem to interest him even though I spent several days at home crying and refusing to return to school. My mother tried to motivate me and told me to look beyond the setback, but I couldn't help but feel like a failure. "I was always the top of the class, Mama. Now, I'm tenth! It doesn't matter how hard I study. I'm never going to rank higher than tenth."

Ramzi did his best to console me. When we were alone, he explained that advanced classes were nothing like the classes in middle school. Some of the girls had been to the Lycée, Notre Dame, The English School, etc., and they were smart. Everything I thought I knew about private-school dimwits went out the window. If you want to succeed in the advanced classes, you have to do more than study, he explained. "You need a stable environment, too, and you and I don't have that. Think about the girls at the top of your class. They're all from well-off, stable families, and they haven't had to deal with the problems we have. That's what it takes to be at the top of the class, whether we like it or not. I'm barely passing my exams in med school. Our environment is crap. It's a miracle we haven't given up." I found Ramzi's rationalization appealing and persuasive. The following term, I did well enough to be ranked eighth in the class, and I didn't feel bad about it at all because I had thoroughly embraced my role as victim.

3

We eventually become the parts we play—fate granting us the roles we're keen to accept. Act a martyr, enjoy the suffering. Shortly before the beginning of my second year of high school, my father was struck with vomiting and diarrhea that just wouldn't stop. Ramzi went to fetch the doctor, so it was just us left in the house: me, my mother, and him. As my mother led him to the bathroom, I tried to make myself scarce, but she started shouting for me—screaming, really, so I ran back and caught him just as he was about to fall. He was naked from the waist down, and his small member was stuck to his thigh. I don't know if he even realized what was happening, but my mother—paragon of tenderness—soothed him, "You have nothing to be embarrassed about. She's your daughter." We helped him over to the daybed near the bathroom, and my mother covered him with a blanket because it was winter and he was shivering. He was trying to say something, but his speech was so slurred I couldn't make anything out. "I forgive you," my mother said. "I forgive you. All is forgiven. I forgive you, my love." He wasn't looking at her, though. I know for certain he was looking at me. He was trying to tell me something, but I couldn't figure it out.

4

When Ramzi got home, he got our father settled into his own bed, and he and Mama sat with him until the doctor arrived. I stepped away. A little while later, the doctor came and went, and then I watched as Ramzi and Mama escorted Father to the neighbor's car. "The doctor said he only has a few hours left," my mother said, but she and Ramzi were going to give it one last shot. When they got to Heliopolis Hospital, Ramzi informed the intake doctor that he was a medical student, so the man graciously followed him out to the car.

"I suggest you take him back home and make him comfortable." Mama told me that Dad had been holding her hand on the drive to the hospital and that he felt cold, but she didn't want to believe it. "I'm very sorry for your loss," the doctor said.

5

I didn't want to say goodbye, but I had no choice. I'd already seen enough for one night—more than my brother had for sure. When I kissed my father's forehead as I'd been instructed, I saw him look back at me, but Mama and Ramzi denied it. "Dad is dead and his eyes are shut. You're just imagining things." I didn't believe them, not least because the following night, Dad knocked on my bedroom door, insistently, until I woke up. The first thing I did in the morning was run to Ramzi's room in a panic to ask if he was the one who'd been knocking on my door before dawn. I questioned my mother, too. Night after night, my father spoke to me through the closed door, repeating those same slurred words I'd struggled to make out as he was dying; I never once dared open it. Eventually, he stopped coming, and he hasn't been back since.

6

The morning after he died, I was sent to a friend's house so that I wouldn't see the preparations for burial, and by the time I returned home, his body was gone. I threw myself on the ground, weeping, and my mother wailed, "What's going to happen to us" as our women neighbors tried to calm us down.

One of them picked me up roughly and said, "Don't ever plant your face in the ground, do you understand me?"

The worst was yet to come, however. Only the family and a few close friends knew the real cause of death. The doctor, who'd foreseen how things would play out even before Ramzi and Mama took Dad to the hospital, was sensitive to our grieving family's trauma and our anxiety about gossip.

Cause of death: Cardiac event.

We all went along with it.

The aftermath: Ramzi, "Daddy's favorite" (our childhood taunt) and the closest to him out of all his kids, cried constantly. I experienced a guilt so deep that my mother spent years trying to free me from it. "I used to pray for him to die every single day. You don't think I have any responsibility for his death?"

I didn't take my exams at the end of the year. I'd fallen so far behind that I was at the bottom of the advanced class and the principal was threatening to move me to a lower group. In the past, you'd have had to tear the book out of my hands to get me to stop studying, but after our father died, all I wanted to do was watch television. I took three of my exams and skipped the other three, so by all accounts I should have been forced to repeat the year, but my Arabic teacher—a poetry-lover—went to the administration and explained what I'd been going through. So—on the basis of his signed affidavit!—they allowed me to re-take the three exams that I'd missed. When he heard that I was planning to skip the exams for a second time, he called me at the house. "Are you trying to send me to jail, young lady? I put my neck on the line for you." I cried, but I kept my word and went to take the exams. I passed and put year two behind me.

7

My mother became very frail in the years that followed because she stopped eating as much so that there would be more food left for us. I still remember a sweet carrot that she'd taken a bite out of before setting it aside so that Ramzi and I could share it when we got home from school. Nothing made her happier than to watch us eat, pray for us, and be surrounded by her "tribe" as she used to call us. Her favorite brother's suicide had been hard on her, and she'd fallen out with the other one, so all she had left was her older sister, my aunt. They remained close—despite being very different or perhaps because they were—for the rest of her life. After Ragi left, she was struck with tapeworm, which never really went away despite the treatment, and then after my father died, she had a series of fractures in her hands and feet, which happened so often that it became a family joke.

My mother's life was punctuated by dramatic twists: her sons were troubled—and look the daughter isn't far behind!—she'd been rich and become poor, she'd fallen in love with someone she shouldn't have fallen in love with and escaped it by marrying someone else, and then when that failed, she'd married my father.

My father was in a bad place, too, when the future couple met. He dreamed of marrying my mother, with whom he shared a distant family connection and the same hometown, but he'd already had to give up on one dream. Instead of studying engineering like he'd always wanted, he enrolled in the institute for middle-school teachers so that he could support his family and so that his younger brother could fulfill his own dream of becoming an engineer and eventually the CEO of a large company.

There was no way he was going to get her. Her father, a wealthy shop owner, doted on her noticeably more than her siblings, and her mother adored her. Meanwhile, his own father was a humble merchant who'd had to declare bankruptcy after the first downturn.

She'd studied in French-language elementary schools before joining the Saneya High School for Girls, but she left education after the second year of high school when she received her diploma. Not for her the baccalaureate, followed by university—even though her father tried to push for it. And it wasn't because she couldn't cut it. She was just spoiled. She wanted to laze around and write poems.

Her older sister couldn't have been more different. She worked hard—not that anyone noticed or cared—and enrolled in the teachers college, later graduating with honors and giving her English teachers a reason to celebrate. It's true that she didn't work after she got married to another teacher from the same college, but together they were able to save and build a nest egg—insulating themselves from her wealthy father's bad luck—that they used to buy a beautiful house with a garden in a posh neighborhood. Bearing the flame of high achievement, their children didn't just study engineering—they got PhDs in the subject. My aunt was a stern and occasionally even cruel mother, but her children worshipped her, which was something my mother found strange and depressing. Especially if my aunt or one of my mother's friends made a rude remark about us falling on hard times or my mother's shabby appearance. In the past, she would get all the latest designs made for her by a famous Greek seamstress, but all she had left was a single dress that she wore year after year. The other women criticized her for spoiling her children until we'd gone rotten.

Her wealthy father had lost his fortune after a poorly judged stock-market caper, so he had to sell everything he owned—"except for his name"—in order to pay off his debts and avoid bankruptcy. From that point on, he became more violent toward my grandmother when he'd been drinking. According to my mother, she was the only one of her siblings who ever stood up to their father when he'd hit their mother. "I dare you to lay a hand on her again," she'd say, which would cause him to break down and back off, filling the house with drunken weeping as he raved about all that he'd lost.

Having decided that she couldn't stand to live with her parents any longer, she agreed to marry the first man who proposed even though she was in love with someone else because it was an unmarriageable kind of love. In my mother's version of events, her new husband was never the villain. He loved her, and she felt that she loved him back while also trying to move past her doomed romance. It was her sisters-in-law who ruined everything. She followed her new husband, a prosecutor and only son, back to his family home in Minya, where his sisters ganged up on her, treating her like "a second wife" and causing him "to turn against her." The marriage ended shortly after that in a nasty divorce.

A photo of my mother and her dashing groom hangs in my house to this very day. I never met the man, but I always wished that he'd been my father. Perhaps only because I don't have any other photos of my mother in a wedding dress. I don't even know if she wore one for her second wedding.

My grandmother had already moved out by the time my newly divorced mother moved back into the family home. During one of my grandfather's blowups, my grandmother, a woman of character and pedigree, had given him an ultimatum: "If you hit me, I swear to God I'll leave," and because my mother hadn't been there to get between them, she moved out the very same day. She was the first woman in my family to leave her husband and live on her own, although they never officially divorced. She didn't seem particularly upset about it, and she even took the young maid with her when she left. Having tolerated her husband for her whole adult life, she figured she couldn't keep it up in old age. My mother divided her time between both parents in short stints, but she got the impression, she later told me, that her father wanted to die alone. My grandmother had two brothers, who supported her very generously after she moved out. They'd both gone by steamship to study medicine in England and had returned to make their fortunes, which they combined with their inheritances, which hadn't been squandered.

My father turned up regularly after my mother's divorce on the pretext of checking in on my grandmother, who was fond of him. Both their lives had changed so much. My father had divorced his first wife after only a few months. People said that he'd caught her cheating, but he didn't kill her or create a scandal—it was all hush-hush. Later, I learned that he had never loved her, but it destroyed him all the same. Betrayed by a woman he'd saved from the streets, or so the rumor went. The old flame began to flicker once more, and why not? With my grandmother's blessing and my preoccupied grandfather's indifference, he proposed to my mother, and they were married.

Embracing her downward mobility and acknowledging that things would never be as good as they had once been—coming to terms with destiny, in other words—my mother accepted the proposal. That's how I like to imagine it because, of course, I wasn't alive then, but the stories I heard growing up did make them sound like a good match. They had hardship in common, and if it hadn't been for my father's jealousy, which led him to distrust her at times—something she felt was completely unjustified—they'd have had a pleasant life. Photos taken around the time my father got his first overseas assignment in Libya make the small family—husband, wife, and two young boys—seem comfortable and well established. Enough to own an electric refrigerator, which they were sure to feature in all their photos.

If only it hadn't been for Ragi, their oldest. According to my mother, Dad had been cruel to Ragi ever since he was a child, and that made her want to indulge him all the more. She couldn't stand to see her two sons treated differently. My guess is that my father had suspicions about my mother's first love because he never got over his first wife's infidelity. In all fairness, the black-and-white photos do support my mother's version of events. There are several photos of my father with his arms around Ramzi, Ragi shoved to one side as he gazes back at them. He hadn't even turned six.

When my grandmother was diagnosed with bone cancer, my mother rushed back from Libya and was told that it was aggressive and that nothing could be done. All she could do was scream, she said. "God help us! She hid it from me for so long!" Ragi was nearly ten, Ramzi was eight, and she'd been pregnant with me for about a month.

My grandmother gathered that my mother was pregnant, so she asked, and my mother responded that she was planning to get an abortion "as usual." My grandmother pleaded with her—"Not this time, Suad. Keep it for my sake." How could she have refused a deathbed wish?

"OK, Mama. If it's a girl, I'll call her Fatma."

My grandmother shut her eyes as if the pain had vanished. "I like the sound of that."

Eight months later, I came into the world, welcomed by my grandmother's dying wish and her name. My mother had spent her entire pregnancy wearing black, sitting in one spot, crying, and hardly eating because my grandmother died a few days after she'd asked her to keep me. I was nourished on tears and crumbs.

8

For once, my mother put her foot down. She insisted that we keep Father's death a secret from Ragi. She was the only one who took his claims of homesickness seriously, and she wouldn't be swayed by the photos we received of his life with his German friends in their dormitory—Ragi painting a wall and smiling, Ragi and his friends seated at a long, stylish dining table having breakfast, etc. He'd been away for three years, during which we'd foregone all his favorite activities, like barbecuing at Eid al-Adha, in order to avoid reminding her of his absence, but she had strong feelings about what had to be done. "If he comes back, he'll have to do military service, and he only has a high school diploma, so he'll go in as a private. It'll destroy him. It's lucky I managed to get him out at all." All those years of entreating neighborhood bureaucrats with sob stories and bribes had worn her out.

A few months later, Ragi heard the news of our father's death from a friend—the same friend who'd encouraged him to go to Germany in the first place. Ragi's friend had married a German woman twice his age, which gained him residency and eventually a German passport, and that was precisely what my mother encouraged Ragi to do. "It's not my style," he said, settling the matter. His friend, who managed a carpet shop and had a knack for business, lived in Frankfurt in a beautiful apartment owned by his wealthy wife, who worked for German intelligence. He and Ragi drifted apart, but that was Ragi's doing. He had decided that he didn't want any Arab friends at all because he wanted to live as a German through and through, having become fluent in the language in just a few years.

He wrote home less often after Dad died. It was as if the only reason he'd been sending letters was to prove to our father that he could fulfill their shared dream of becoming an engineer. "My boy's studying to be an engineer. And in Germany of all places!" Father loved to say.

The things he wrote made our mother uneasy because she was the only one who really understood him and his tricks, but we told her she was being maudlin for no good reason. She had never got over him leaving and was always anxious about what he'd make of himself. I kept telling her not to be distrustful and pessimistic—Ramzi and I both told her that. Eventually, she stopped telling us that she felt scared and upset, and always did her best to act cheerful in front of us. Just a few years ago, I was looking through her old notebooks, which I'd brought with me from the old house, when I came across a small notebook that I'd never laid eyes on. My mother had never shared any of her writing with me, so I burst into tears when I read her description of the torment that Ragi's departure had caused and how hard it had been to have to hide it from us. My mother took refuge in writing—as I've done for years, as I'm doing now.

I couldn't face high school anymore after the disaster of my second year, so I went to pay Ragi a surprise visit. His old friend was back in Cairo for a short trip, and he was the one who suggested it. "She'll get to see her brother and take her mind off things, Auntie. One year won't make a difference either way. I'm planning to take my sister back to Germany with me, too." My mother bought me a one-way ticket so that I could travel with them, but it stretched her. The only way she could afford it was to join a savings group.

Nothing beats a mother's intuition. Ragi, who was shocked to see me, had no choice but to come clean about the mess he was in. His documents had been discovered to be fake, so the university had given him a couple of months' warning before he was expelled, including from the dorms. He worked two days a week to pay for his meals and spent the rest of his time in bed. He couldn't face the debts that he owed people and he begged me not to tell anyone—definitely not our mother or Ramzi. Nor any of the other Arabs who lived in his small town and were doing everything they could to get to know me, the lovely young Arab girl who'd just arrived. He didn't even want me to tell his old friend, whom he was angry at for bringing me there.

The days I spent in that tiny dorm room were the worst days of my life. Months later, with no prospect of ever earning enough to buy me a ticket back home, Ragi sent our mother a letter in which he told her the truth. He said that she and Ramzi could never understand what he was going through, and he chided them for sending him another mouth to feed.

My mother was horrified. She immediately booked a plane ticket for me, and when she met me at the airport, she couldn't stop touching my body and crying. I was twice as heavy as I'd been when I left. "What happened to you? Are you okay?" For months, all I'd had to eat was stale bread and scraps of cheese that the German students would leave for me in the refrigerator when they went back home over the weekend. I spent the entire time either in Ragi's room or in the kitchen, and I was always careful not to be seen by anyone other than the students—who were sympathetic to our situation—so that we wouldn't get thrown out.

I couldn't bring myself to tell my mother everything that had happened. Not even when she asked me about the cut on my left wrist, which still hadn't healed. I did tell Ramzi, though. He cried and held me as he listened to me talk about trying to kill myself while I was there because of how Ragi treated me and because I didn't want to have to tell our mother what had happened to him. Ramzi encouraged me to keep it a secret from our mother, and I agreed that I needed to turn the page.

Before I could, though, I wanted Ramzi to help me write a letter to Ragi so I could tell him how he'd made me feel. He used to leave me without any money for days and had forbidden me from writing to our mother to ask for help. There were nights he wouldn't let me sleep. "Solitary confinement," I called it. Trying to stay awake for hours in the dim light of a lamp I propped up on the sink in our room. Ragi asleep on the other side of the curtain that he hung to divide the room in two. It was my job to stay awake until dawn so that I could wake him up for work. Were I to fail, he wouldn't go, and we wouldn't eat for the rest of the week. When I tried to kill myself, all he said to me was, "Is that all you care about? You just wanna die? Well, go die somewhere else. I have enough to worry about already." My mother didn't know that I sent him the letter, "The Vendetta Letter" Ramzi and I called it, which ended with the sentence: "You're not my brother anymore, and I never want to see you again." Ragi replied with a short apology for how he'd behaved, but I never forgave him for it. Even now as I write this, I can't face the memory. I strain to push it beyond the boundaries of my recollection.

9

He disappeared after that—stopped sending letters and calling. It made my mother cry, but no one else. Whenever she met someone coming back from Germany, she'd ask them if they knew Ragi and gave them cassettes to take back with them in case they bumped into him in the street. On the cassettes, she begged him to speak to her. It was torture for a mother not to know if her child was even alive. Ragi's old friend who used to give us updates had cut ties with him, but he reassured my mother that Ragi was still alive and that if anything ever happened to him, he would hear about it.

We didn't hear from him again for years. Not until he bumped into that same old friend in a train station and heard that Ramzi was working as a doctor in Saudi Arabia. He called the house when Ramzi was back in Cairo on vacation, but since both he and my mother were out, I was the one who answered the phone. I was thrilled to hear his voice, and it felt like all the old hurts had vanished. I'd grown older, and I'd been through worse. He asked me to tell Ramzi to call him back urgently at the number of a girlfriend, but when I told him he should call back a little later because our mother was desperate to speak to him, his tone changed. "No, not Mama. I don't want to deal with emotions. Goodbye." First shock, then the old anger erupted.

I didn't tell my mother—as she jumped with joy and thanked God for protecting her son—how the phone call had ended. I went over every last detail of the phone call for her dozens of times, but never the last thing he'd said. I couldn't imagine telling my mother that her son had refused to speak to her after all those years, but all she seemed to care about was that she finally knew he was alright.

Ragi, having long abandoned his dream of becoming an engineer, convinced Ramzi that they should go into business together refurbishing and selling old cars. Ramzi and his wife were excited at the prospect, so he sent Ragi five hundred dollars to get started, and they agreed to split the profits. They used to speak on the phone, but Ramzi kept that a secret from our mother. Ramzi was very patient, as his wife indulged fantasies of becoming wealthier, but then Ragi disappeared again. Ramzi lost his dollars, and—in order to placate his wife—he lost his brother, too, although he did try to make excuses for him at first by alluding to difficult circumstances. His justifications were full of the old affection that had once made them so close that people thought they were twins, but they couldn't withstand his wife's blunt "Your brother ripped you off." His conflicted feelings were resolved in an instant.

10

Because we rarely ever had guests in the house besides Ramzi's friends, my mother was surprised to find a man at our front door asking to see my father to discuss "a family matter." My girlfriends weren't allowed to come over—"Their house is full of young men," their families said. I could understand why that made them wary, so I would go over to their houses instead. My father wasn't very gregarious, and he often invented excuses to sabotage my mother's attempts to have people over and be hosted in return. "Whenever we had guests, he'd charm their socks off, but he lacked confidence. As soon as they left, he'd say, 'I can't take any more socializing, please.'"

The stranger appeared at our doorstep a few months before Father died. When Ramzi, who was studying in his bedroom with a friend, caught sight of the man, he appeared to get irritated and quickly shut the door. Mama and I eavesdropped as the man explained to our father that Ramzi had gone to his house more than a week ago to ask for permission to marry his daughter! The man told Ramzi to come back with his parents, and he promised that he would, but when he failed to turn up, the man decided to come speak to his father to find out what was going on.

Our father reacted very calmly and decided that he would lie. He told the girl's father that Ramzi had spoken to him about wanting to get engaged, and he assured him that Ramzi was a fine young man. He invented a whole conversation in which he'd counseled Ramzi to reconsider his plans and wait until he'd finished the third year of medical school before getting engaged.

My mother and I couldn't believe Father was being so cool about the delicate situation. After agreeing that their families would soon meet, the man left, and my red-faced father went into Ramzi's bedroom. The friend who'd been over studying escaped through the balcony, leaving father and son to speak in hushed tones that my mother and I couldn't make out. Not that it mattered. We observed the conversation's effect on Ramzi's mood in the days that followed.

My mother was so irate that she refused to speak to him. She simply couldn't believe that Ramzi was thinking about getting married before he'd even graduated from medical school and before his family had seen any benefit from the medical career that they'd worked so hard to make possible.

"It's like the scene in Naguib Mahfouz's *The Beginning and the End* when Hassanein proposes to Bahia," was my mother's caustic description, but of course she had no idea how prescient she was. Ramzi holed up in his bedroom for days listening to Abdel Halim sing, "One day, one month, one year from now, this pain will heal" over and over again. He even wrote the lyrics out by hand and stuck them on his bedroom door, but our mother didn't take pity on him like she normally would have. She wouldn't forgive him. She wouldn't even hear him out even though she used to listen to Ragi rant for hours. "She took his feelings seriously, but not mine," was how he put it to me later.

11

I didn't take his feelings seriously either because I knew the girl he was infatuated with. She was in the final year of middle school, and at one point, he'd said he would stop riding the tram with me on our way to school and university, respectively, unless she could join us. He used to sit across from her and stare while she pretended to be flustered.

Her awkwardness was really just a performance. I knew because I used to see her in the tramcar on my way back home, too. I was always in my secondary school uniform—buttoned all the way up to the collar—and wearing a tie I'd taken from my father's collection while she was dressed in an unbuttoned shirt, her hair hanging loose, and she and her friends laughed so loud that all the passengers could hear them. They went to a co-ed private school in Midan Hegaz that had a bad reputation. She and her friends constantly made fun of my austere uniform and heavy bookbag, and I can still picture her now, pointing at me, with nothing more than a notebook and textbook in one hand.

I watched her gesture to him from her bedroom window as he and his friends played football in the street outside, having only recently moved the location of their matches. That was why Maha had broken up with him, I realized. Maha, whom we'd loved and who'd become part of the family, was gone forever.

12

The girl's mother and father were the first people to come pay their respects after our father's death, even though our families hadn't been in touch at all since the surprise visit. Ramzi had managed to pass his third year exams, re-taking only two—"despite the stress of losing a parent," he noted—and he eventually wore our mother down, so she agreed that the pair could get engaged and exchange rings. The girl's uncle on her mother's side who called the shots in their family did try to intervene—"Why would we let her marry someone who still gets an allowance from his mother?"—but Ramzi won him over with his sincere determination: "I'm going to be a doctor, and I'm going to be rich. You'll see. I'm going to make her the happiest woman on earth!" It wasn't easy to pretend that he didn't feel insulted, he later told me, but they agreed to table the question of money for the time being.

It was settled and, despite my and my mother's misgivings, the two families paid each other formal visits. It was at that point that our mother insisted that Ramzi make time for me. "You have to take your sister out, just the two of you, like you used to, twice a month." He agreed immediately, and we did go out together once, but after that, he acted resentful about the promise he'd made, so I decided to let him off the hook and save myself the hours I wasted each time he stood me up.

I can see now that the problems I faced in high school had nothing to do with being tenth in my advanced class. My father had died, and Ragi was no longer a part of my life, so the only one left was Ramzi, and we were as close as could be before he was snatched away by romance.

When we went to visit his fiancée's family, the three of us—Ramzi, Mama, and me—would stay past midnight. Ramzi blocked out our mother's many signals that it was time for us to be going—"Oh, it's got so late," etc., ignored everyone yawning even. All he did was look at the girl adoringly as if she were the only person in the world.

Late at night as the three of us made our way home, he'd stop in the middle of the road and tell us he had to go back. He'd detected sorrow in her eyes as he was leaving! My mother tutted. "Fine, but you're going to take us home first. I'm sure you weren't planning to abandon your mother and sister in the street after midnight!"

Swept away by a strong current, she was the only thing he could still see on shore. A lifeline in the distance.

13

I told Ramzi I wanted to start smoking. He'd been engaged for a few weeks by then, so I was being deliberately provocative. "I swear if I ever catch you with a cigarette, I'll put it out on your face."

Everyone in the house smoked except for me, but that wasn't what made me say it. In addition to the formal visits our families exchanged, Ramzi's fiancée used to come over to the house, and I would see them go into his bedroom and shut the door. Then when he opened it again, I'd catch a glimpse of her lying on the bed as playful and passionate Ramzi lit her cigarette.

She was younger than me, but only by a few months, and she was beautiful. They'd spend the afternoons together at our house, Ramzi making her cups of tea and sandwiches, and whenever my mother nagged him to "pay some attention to your sister," it only led to more conflict.

In the end, I bought myself a pack of cigarettes and then promptly confessed to my mother. "Mama, I've started smoking, and I didn't want to lie to you." She didn't say anything. She just looked at me, and then offered me one of hers. Side by side, we smoked together in silence.

14

Then the girl ended it. On the night before his final-year exams, she came over to tell Ramzi that she didn't love him. He knew she was lying, but she gave the ring back all the same. We heard rumors that her family had set her up with her cousin—her father's brother's son—who'd been working as a physician for a few years already and owned his own apartment and clinic. Some families prefer relatives to strangers.

But that wasn't the real reason. She'd already admitted to him that she wasn't interested in her cousin. No; an old flame, whom Ramzi knew about and thought he'd thoroughly supplanted, had resurfaced.

Ramzi took his broken heart to Alexandria. Even though Mama and I tried to hide it, we couldn't help but feel relieved, and Ramzi knew he wasn't likely to get much sympathy from us. He stayed there until the exam period was over, and the whole time he was away, our mother paced around the house saying things like, "Couldn't that little bitch have at least waited until his exams were over? She'll get what's coming to her one day." Ramzi had to repeat his fourth year as expected, but we were so happy to see him when he came back from Alexandria, it felt like it had all been a dream.

15

As the months went by, Ramzi appeared to forget all about her. He was preoccupied with my friend Hiyam, who was several years older than me and both married and a flirt. Her husband worked abroad, and they were "separated," according to her, but they didn't want to get divorced for the sake of their children. She used to tell me about her adventures and always seemed to have someone new on hand, like our teenage neighbor who I used to play with when we were kids. He'd started taking dixies, which made him violent and erratic. After he beat up his mother and sister, he went upstairs to Hiyam's apartment so she could calm him down. The following morning, she described his muscles and youthful body to me.

We were very different people, but I liked her a lot. She never tried to draw me into her way of life because she understood that I was much younger and lacked any real experience. She wasn't particularly beautiful, but she was lighthearted. She used to tell jokes that filled the air around her like colorful balloons, and I found myself laughing non-stop whenever we were together.

When she opened up to me about her latest love affair, I was taken aback because I'd never known her to be so romantic. "He's the first man I've ever truly loved," she said. She was going to make big changes just for him: divorce her husband, follow him anywhere, stop fooling around. I had to ask her who the mystery man was several times, but eventually her resolve crumbled and she told me what had been going on behind my back between her and my brother. All I could do was laugh. When I saw Ramzi again after I got back home, I laughed some more, and then things went back to normal between us, like they'd always been.

16

When I got older, I began to understand why our mother felt she was on the edge of a precipice. She used to take me with her when she went to visit her father's brother, an elegant and imposing man who had tried to reconcile her and her brother and who only very occasionally visited us at home, and his wife Tante Jilan, who never visited us at home but always embraced my mother when we went to see them at their large, high-ceilinged apartment in the Korba district. The one with the balcony so huge that I was allowed to ride around it on a bike. My mother liked to go by tram when we went to visit them. We'd either get off one stop before or, if I had my way, at Roxy, where I'd beg her to buy me a candied apple from the Greek vendor who stood outside Sednaoui's department store. I used to devour it like it was ice cream. She would insist that we walk through the neighborhood and would remind me—for the thousandth time—that the street we were on was named after her relative Abdel Salam Gardanah in recognition of his engineering genius.

On other occasions that I found the most fun, we used to go visit my mother's cousin Tante Nana at her apartment in Zamalek. She and my mother had been very close as children and knew the secrets of each other's first loves. I knew her as a dark and beautiful woman who was married to a famous doctor. She prepared little sachets of chocolates and candies for my visits and would reveal them one after the other in a series of surprises. Still, I couldn't help but feel intimidated when we sat at the dining table and were waited on by a butler dressed in a white galabiyya and red belt.

My mother repeated in a whisper everything that she and Tante Sharifa had taught me: use a knife and fork and chew with your mouth closed. I used to eat like that at home sometimes, so it wasn't particularly difficult, but it was stressful to eat at Tante Nana's house. I was so worried that I'd make a faux pas that I only ate the dishes that I knew weren't going to pose a challenge. Always passing on mouthwatering fried chicken because it took real skill to eat it with a knife and fork and not make a mess. I pretended not to like it, and my mother backed me up.

She and Tante Nana shared a deep bond. I have a photo of the two of them as children with their arms around each other, which I can remember my mother looking at from time to time. "People used to say that I was the prettiest. That I'd land a better husband than the rest of the girls."

Our visits grew less frequent and eventually ceased entirely. I didn't see Tante Nana or any of my mother's relatives for years until they came to pay their respects when my father died. They turned up in fancy chauffeur-driven cars, offered condolences, and were off again in no time. That was the last time I saw them.

When I got older, my mother explained to me that she was the one who'd drifted away from Tante Nana. She got tired of bumping into relatives and childhood friends whenever she went over to her house. She couldn't bear the looks of disbelief and pity they gave her when they saw her faded dress and cracked shoes, which she tried to hide under the table. It didn't make a difference how much Tante Nana defended her for sacrificing so much for her children and enduring a marriage none of them could even imagine; she still felt demeaned.

She cut ties with all of them without the slightest regret—perhaps even with some relief. Apart from anything else, the only thing that mattered to her was her little tribe of three kids. We were the entire world to her. She often spoke to us about the sacrifices she'd made, but we either ignored her or made jokes, which even she laughed at. Whenever she bought anything new for herself, she felt compelled to provide a long list of justifications. Once, when I was an adult, she showed me a pair of her crumbling shoes to prove that she wasn't being profligate because she'd brought home a new cheap and shiny pair. "Mama, you don't need to go to court each time your shoes fall apart and you need a new pair. You're allowed to buy things for yourself. I'm happy for you," I told her, avoiding the temptation to turn the moment into a joke. She smiled and appeared to realize that I'd grown up and could finally understand. She wore her new shoes around the house all day "to break them in," she claimed.

17

I loved going to visit my grandfather on my dad's side. I have a photo of him dressed in an elegant suit with a fez perched on his head, appearing formidable, but that wasn't how I knew him. For years after his business went belly up, he lay in bed playing up his paralysis, so my father had to give up his dream of becoming an engineer and start working to support the family.

With its fusty linoleum floor, my grandfather's bedroom looked out over the mausoleums around the El-Sayyida Aisha Mosque. I used to throw open the shutters in the daytime to watch the funeral processions going past, and at night, I'd cast my eyes over the grave markers. Perhaps because I'm so accustomed to the sight of death, it's never frightened me, but I may have encountered it more than I should have. I'm always there when death appears, there to see the final moments, and when it comes time to wash the body, the deceased's family and friends always look so embarrassed when they try to catch my eye, especially if I didn't really know the person, but I volunteer nonetheless. Most people find the ritual terrifying, but I feel at ease with the dead. I know to treat them tenderly and kiss their shrouded faces.

Whenever the metro went past, my grandfather's building used to shake violently, but we knew it would never collapse. There were broken steps on the staircase you had to leap over before reaching his damp apartment on the second floor, where there was only a squat toilet. The small gap beneath the bathroom door always let in a draft, which I enjoyed feeling on my bare butt.

My grandmother used to come visit us at our house wearing a black galabiyya and headscarf. When she was ready to leave, I'd walk with her to the bus stop, where she'd sit on the curb while she waited. I'd stroll around a little, and by the time I circled back, she'd be sitting on the bus, and my assignment would be over. She was an extremely beautiful woman, and people were always turning their heads to look at her when she walked past. She had green eyes, and her blond hair fell over her shoulders and showed through the mesh of her loosely tied headscarf. My grandfather was good-looking, too, and when I was younger, I thought he was the ultimate embodiment of the patriarch character in Mahfouz's *Palace Walk*. Whenever he called for my grandmother, she'd drop whatever she was doing and rush over. My mother would sometimes block her path just for fun. "Why doesn't he just go get it himself? Can't he walk? I'm not letting you past." But my nervous grandmother would slip away, breaking into a run when she heard her name: "Zahira! Where are you, girl?"

There were no chocolates at my grandparents' house, but I did spend a lot of time with my grandmother and aunt in the kitchen preparing meals. They always put me in charge of making something all by myself. I learned to make doll-shaped pies, and I knew just how much water and vinegar to add to the tahini so that it wouldn't break.

My aunt Ihsan had elephantiasis and heart problems so she never left the house. All she could do was carry her fleshy body from one room to the other, panting. I thought she'd never got married, but when I was older I found out that she'd got married in secret to a married man, whom she loved. My mother was the only person whom Aunt Ihsan trusted enough to confide in. She treated me like a daughter, and not just me—all the kids in the family were like her kids. She spent long afternoons with my grandmother in the kitchen pitting olives, stuffing them with precise slivers of carrot, pickling lemons, packing them with safflower. Filling jar after jar, each headed to a different home.

After she became an adult, my youngest aunt, Nahed, did all the heavy lifting. She was as beautiful as my grandmother, but even more daring and fun, and with her looks and personality, to me, she was like Nadia Lotfy. She rode the bus wearing short, sleeveless dresses that were fashionable at the time and would smoke openly in public. All it took was a single joke—or sometimes an arch comment—to charm everyone on the bus. Beautiful and down to earth. Even taxi drivers loved her. She used to bargain with them over the fare mercilessly when she got back home, but then she'd ask them to wait downstairs so she could send down a tray of delicious food. They'd rub their hands together excitedly and praise her generosity between mouthfuls.

She married a famous journalist and moved out of the family home near the El-Sayyida Aisha Mosque into a grand apartment in Garden City. She truly loved her husband, who was twice her age, and bore him daughters and a son. She'd always assumed that he'd die before her, but, in the end, he lived on for several more heartbroken years. Neither of them had recovered after death drowned their son. For the rest of her life, my aunt's moods swung wildly, and her thoughts were always somewhere else.

18

My father's brother's house was lovely, too. It wasn't elegant like the houses of my mother's relatives, but it was laid out in the classic style with solid and expensive furniture from Damietta, the city that both sides of our family hailed from. His work had taken him to Alexandria, and going to visit him there was always a special treat. My mother and I would go for two or three days at most—"Let's not overstay our welcome," she'd say—which was very unlike our long sojourns at Umm Fuad's house in Suez. My father never joined us—not at his parents' house or his brother's house. He would occasionally drop by to see his sister Ihsan briefly because she was the only one who couldn't come to us, but my grandmother and Aunt Nahed came to our house regularly. Now I understand that he was trying to avoid my grandfather because he never forgave him for tying him to a bedpost and beating him with a belt so that he'd grow into a man. And he never forgave him for destroying his dream of becoming an engineer by "pretending to be crippled," as he used to say.

After he became a CEO, and after my father had hit him up for money one too many times, my uncle started visiting less often and eventually stopped. "I sacrificed my entire life so that he could get a good education," I heard my father ranting to my mother once. "Now he says he'll only lend me money if I give him an IOU, the son of a bitch!"

19

We didn't see our uncle again until our father's funeral. My mother told Ramzi to be nice to him, but as usual, he took dad's side, so she gave him a quick talking to: "You're the man of the house now. Whatever problems your dad and his brother had were between them, and it's none of your business. He's still your uncle. And anyway, your sister deserves to have a family." Later, when my uncle leaned over to tell Ramzi exactly how much he'd spent on our father's funeral, Ramzi stormed over to our mother to tell her what had happened. She couldn't believe it.

"I'm so ashamed I just want to throw the money back in his face!"

"He would never take a cent from you," my mother said. "And, believe me, it won't make a difference. The man has no shame. Let's just get through tonight."

I didn't see my uncle again for another twenty years. Not until my mother's funeral. Cars pulled up outside our house and out came an elderly man and his elderly wife plus her sister and their two daughters with their husbands and their son with his wife, and suddenly the house was crammed. I searched my cousins' faces for any sign of my childhood friends—my old playmates and beach buddies. "Come on, go get packed," my uncle said to me. "I'll wait for you." I had no idea what he was talking about. "You'll come stay with us now. You can't be on your own, and you're always welcome at your uncle's house."

The expression "your uncle's house" simply didn't compute. It came from a different planet, a different tongue. It took me a second to find the words to respond.

"I'm sorry, Uncle, but I've got my studies to focus on." It sounded strange to me as soon as I said it—my studies! I sounded like a child, and I'd walked right into his trap, embracing the role he'd forced on me. He was my uncle and I was his brother's daughter—a little girl. The only thing stopping me from going with him was that I had to study.

"Just bring your books," he said. "We'll wait for you."

"No, no, I can't. My life is here. It's out of the question," I said, finally finding my voice again.

They wouldn't leave until I promised to think about it. Before I could even ask myself if my father had taken advantage of him or if my mother had been unfair, I watched him walk toward his car, leaning on his cane as the driver opened the door. He sat and lifted his legs before swinging them into the car. He was followed by his wife and her sister, who were leaning on each other for support, but his kids and their partners had already headed straight to their own cars. None of them paid any attention to my uncle, who seemed very old and very alone, and I understood why he'd been so insistent.

Not that I took his invitation seriously. By the evening, it had become a funny story that I shared with my girlfriends. "My uncle turned up out of nowhere expecting me to drop everything and move in with him so I could be his nurse. He thought I'd blow up my whole life in five minutes." I tried to hide the dread I felt with laughter. The dread of having him back in my life. The dread of his pestering in the days to come.

But there was nothing after that. He never visited again, never even called—not him, not his kids—although he'd made such a big show of taking down my number when they came over. He actually repeated it out loud more than once to make sure he'd got it right! He died less than a year after my mother.

20

When Hiyam's husband returned unexpectedly, she agreed to take him back after a lot of talking and sobbing.

She did it for the sake of her "two daughters who are still so little," she explained as she combed her hair, and she was genuinely crying when she asked me if I'd tell Ramzi what fate had wrought and beg him not to be angry.

Fate aside, he was still angry. So angry that he wrote her a nasty letter in which he accused her of betraying him and toying with his emotions. I was asked to deliver it, of course.

When I went over there, Hiyam hugged me and her husband greeted me warmly, as well. The two little girls snuck furtive glances at my handbag because I often brought them chocolates and they'd begun to anticipate a surprise. Now that the separation, which hadn't lasted very long at all, was at an end, the household was joyous, and that was something that Hiyam played up. She took me into her bedroom to show me the gifts her husband had brought her and to ask me how Ramzi had taken the news. It upset her to hear that he was angry, but all she said was, "Pretty soon he'll get married and have kids, and then he'll understand." I didn't give her the letter because it seemed pointless and I felt awkward handing a letter to a woman from her former lover when her husband had just welcomed me into his home with genuine affection.

To me, the situation was as plain as day, and I felt confident about my decision, but when I got home and told Ramzi how happy the whole family was and explained that I couldn't bring myself to give her the letter without talking to him about it first, he completely flipped out. I tried to articulate my ethical stance, but that just aggravated him more. "Do you really think I want her back? Why would I chase after a woman like that? I just want to give her a piece of my mind, and you're refusing to help me retain a shred of dignity. I'm your brother!"

He gave me the silent treatment for more than a month, but then one day, everything went back to normal. This time it wasn't because he'd forgotten why he was angry, but because he'd had several conversations with the mother of his ex-fiancee, Buthayna. She never came to the house, of course, because they didn't want Mama to catch on. Rather, when she walked past the house and spotted Ramzi studying on the balcony with his friends for the fourth-year exams he'd missed after his engagement was called off, she'd wave to him from across the street, and he'd jump down from the balcony to go talk to her. My mother and I were clueless about those meetings, but I did overhear his friends teasing him at one point: "Why does that lady wave at you every day? I don't get it. Does she have a crush on you?"

I told my mother what I'd heard, and she was upset at first, but she decided to ignore it. Right before the exam results came out, Ramzi told us that he was planning to marry Buthayna "We're back together now." The news came as a shock to my mother, who couldn't wait for Ramzi to graduate so that he could help out with the household expenses, if only a bit, but to me it felt like the long-awaited death sentence was finally being carried out.

21

By the time I got back from Germany, the university entrance exams were only two months away. I considered skipping them and starting again from scratch the following year, but my mother had arranged everything while I was away. I had refused to go back to school, so she enrolled me as a remote student, to study by correspondence and she even went to the district office to buy the textbooks I needed. She knew I didn't have enough time to study before the exams, but I also knew that she'd been traumatized by a long string of re-takes.

I studied with half a brain while the other half was busy processing the disastrous trip to Germany and the scar on my wrist. My mother never put any pressure on me to pass. All she said was, "Please just take the test. It doesn't matter if you don't pass." I did pass, though. The old star student in me came out and my result, even though I wasn't very happy with it, was the best of anyone on our street.

The other girls in the advanced classes were going on to become doctors, engineers, and pharmacists, as had been forecast for me not two years earlier, but I didn't dare ask my mother to relive her old nightmare and let me re-take the exam to get a higher score the following year. Whenever I saw an old classmate, I crossed the street so that I wouldn't have to face questions about my old dream of becoming an oncologist. People used to mock me, but I liked to shut them up by saying, "I want to save people from the disease that killed my grandmother."

My role was to pay the price for my brothers' repeated failures and be content with my assignment: College of Arts and Humanities: Psychology. Ramzi tried to persuade me that I could get a clinical diploma after graduation and that being a therapist was just as important as being a doctor; no one cared that my heart wasn't in it.

Everything was on track, it seemed. Ramzi had finally graduated, I was studying psychology, and our mother was content.

22

Eighteen years old, wearing makeup as thick as a mask, I slowly made my way past the sons and daughters of Egypt's upper-middle class, who were sitting beside a path that led to a stand selling drinks and sandwiches run by a man named Jimmy. The boys catcalled me while the girls made comments about the "kilo of makeup" I had on. I didn't have any girlfriends of my own. My only two friends—neighbors since childhood—had got married and moved away that same year. Ra'ifa had yet to appear in my life, and Ramzi had forbidden Hiyam from coming to the house to see me because "it makes Buthayna jealous."

"Are you saying I can't have my friend over because it makes Buthayna feel bad? That's rich. She's going to come over whether you like it or not!" Despite my defiance, Hiyam stayed away after I told her about the fight that I had with Ramzi. Mama even agreed that whoever had a problem with Hiyam coming to visit "could get lost," but I couldn't persuade her to come over again after that.

I failed to make friends during my first year at university. I felt like I'd been through a lot compared to my classmates who seemed like children to me. Had any of them lived abroad? Had any of them spent the night in a train station with nothing between them and the freezing cold but their cheap clothes? Had any of them ever overstayed a visa?

"Don't you dare tell them where you've been this whole time," Ragi said when he dropped me off at the train station on my way to the airport. "I don't want any trouble."

How many of my classmates had spent long layovers in multiple airports on a ticket that their mother could barely afford, being asked insulting questions by the police about why they'd remained in the country illegally? It was a miracle that I'd even made it. They were kids, fresh out of high school, and to them, going to university was an adventure in itself.

I tried to avoid the area around Jimmy's after that, but not because of the comments the girls made about my makeup. Rather, it was my clothing, and specifically my only new dress, which my mother had triumphantly bought for me, which failed to compete against the fashion trends that changed from one day to the next. I was a beautiful young woman, and I knew it.

"She's stuck up," said the girls.

"She has a right to be," the boys retorted with a wink.

23

Ramzi and Buthayna got married a week after his exam results came out. My mother couldn't bear any more of Ramzi's begging, so she gave him our late father's monthly pension and made him swear to return the money as soon as he received cash gifts after the wedding. He bought a bedroom suite on installment, and he and his bride set themselves up in Ragi's old room—the one with the long, snaking balcony that overlooked the street.

There were four of us in the house again, and as usual, we were split into two camps, but this time I wasn't a neutral observer. Where it had once been Ragi and Mama vs Ramzi and Dad, now Mama and I were on the same team.

Our mother waited patiently for Ramzi to repay the money so that she could mend the hole in our monthly finances, but he kept putting it off until he finally confessed that his wife had taken the money and used it to buy gifts for her siblings. "I'm sorry, Mama. I told her it was wrong, but you know how brides can be. Let's just drop it."

We were living off my father's meager pension, so when Ramzi went to do his military service, his wife moved back in with her parents across the street. When he returned, each faction kept their distance. One morning, my mother found jars of urine underneath their bed and surmised that he was so desperate to avoid bumping into either of us that he preferred to pee in a jar at night rather than walk across the apartment. She suggested that he and Buthayna move into the large bedroom at the back of the house next to the bathroom, and he liked that idea. It had been my bedroom, but I didn't mind, and it gave them the option of leaving through the balcony if they didn't want to interact with us.

24

Tante Sharifa's house was always peaceful—if you ignored the whirr of the sewing machine in the daytime.

The place smelled of fabric, but I got used to it and eventually developed an association with it. I got used to the sporadic thwack of the fly-swatter, too, which was adeptly wielded by Sharifa's husband Uncle Salem. He often walked the perimeter of the apartment dressed in striped pajama pants and a bright-white undershirt, hand towel slung over his left shoulder, before retiring to his study in the afternoon. I can't remember him dressed in anything other than house clothes.

The house's large veranda overlooked a garden in one of Cairo's new, tranquil suburbs, and that was usually where we sat when we visited them in summer. One of Tante Sharifa's children—her eldest, Salma, or her son, Shehab—would stop by to chat for a bit before moving on, and they always had a chocolate treat for me.

I preferred to sit out on the veranda with the adults rather than play in the living room by myself because I worried that I'd irritate Tante Sharifa if I messed up the sofas or the dining table, which were always arranged so meticulously. I was allowed to sit at the table in the kitchen, breathing in mouth-watering aromas, and because the kitchen was right next to the front door, I was in prime position to open it if anyone rang the bell.

I didn't like sitting at the dining table with Tante Sharifa's family and especially not when she had lots of relatives over. "Shut your mouth when you're chewing! Hold your fork the right way!" I'm grateful that she took the time to teach me manners, but she was needlessly stern, and she didn't care if she embarrassed me in front of other people. I cried myself to sleep on many nights because of her.

Yet she made up for it by making me gorgeous dresses with the fabric that she had left over from her clients. I loved showing them off to my friends. Once when I was in high school, I told her that I adored all the outfits that Suad Hosny wore in the film *Watch Out for Zouzou*, and when we went to see her the following week, she had dresses hanging up in the sewing room waiting for me. I kissed her over and over again as she laughed and tried to push me off. "That's enough now, girl. I hope you like them."

Both Salma and Shehab dressed elegantly, smelled wonderful, and liked to sprinkle English and French words in their sentences like baubles. Their mother had insisted that her children would attend foreign-language schools, and because she herself had graduated from the Institute of Home Economics, she decided that she'd supplement the household income by working as a seamstress. News of her talent spread quickly through Heliopolis, and her clientele included famous actresses and dancers, so she became very well respected.

Uncle Salem was no slouch, but I think his only source of income was a meager pension from Sudan, where his family still lived. He hadn't seen them since he'd been exiled to Egypt. Despite having no interest in politics, Tante Sharifa fell head over heels for the dashing Sudanese dissident and they got married. Uncle Salem despised Abdel Nasser, which was something he and my father had in common, but he was more vocal about it. Hardly anyone read the articles he wrote, but they still raided Tante Sharifa's house at dawn one morning and took him away. It was a serious crisis. Her friends stopped visiting, the phone stopped ringing, even her clients stayed away for months. New expressions entered the household vocabulary: "Visiting hours," "wiretaps." All I know for certain is that they didn't send him to prison like the other dissidents. Tante Sharifa used to tell us that he enjoyed bantering with the officers. "Come on now, Salem, you're gonna get us all arrested!" I can still remember her venting to my mother about the friends who'd revealed their true colors.

My mother never stopped visiting Tante Sharifa at home even though my father cautioned her against it. She didn't seem to care and, as far as I could tell, he only did it out of a sense of obligation. I think he was secretly proud of her.

It was around then that my mother started talking more openly about her youthful nationalism. She told me about a protest against the British that she'd attended when she was in high school. "Down with the English!" She chanted with the crowd. According to her, she narrowly escaped being trampled by the officers' horses, but I have to admit we were skeptical.

Uncle Salem returned home frail and irascible and spent most of his time alone in his study. Tante Sharifa complained incessantly to my mother, but she put up with it. She also became much more affectionate toward me than she'd been in the past. I loved her, and I knew she loved me, too, in her way. I understood that she was the one keeping my teenage impulses in check, albeit furtively. My mother usually indulged me, but if Tante Sharifa thought something was a bad idea, there was no arguing about it.

Visitors filled the house once more, and bolts of fabric were lined up neatly beside the sewing machine. Tante Sharifa said she was too busy to make any more clothes for me. Her sudden change of heart upset my mother as did her new excuse that she was "too busy working to socialize." Her new friends "had sold her out when she needed them," my mother said, "but now they're back." My mother wanted to open up to her like they'd done so often in the past, but Tante Sharifa had started going out to the cinema and the theatre with her new friends, so she just wanted to talk about the wonderful costumes that the Reda dance troupe had worn the night before or the amazing performances in *My Fair Lady*. They saw less of each other over time but remained friends, and whenever things got bad, they were still each other's first call.

25

Hiyam and I remained friends throughout. She was the one who commiserated with me when I complained about university and the psychology department, but she never came to the house, so we had to schedule dates at her place. She'd begun working at one of the import-export firms that were spreading like wildfire back in the late seventies, and I gathered from some of the things she'd said that she was sleeping with her boss, but she never admitted it. Maybe she was worried that I'd tell Ramzi and open old wounds? Hiyam told me about her boss's numerous adventures with women and about the fancy hotels they'd gone to together when they wanted a break from work, about the beers, conversation, and laughs that they'd shared.

Her husband had begun to sense something, so he asked her to quit her job, and she acceded to his wishes, but she did complain to me about it because she still had to earn a living and now she just had to find another job. My destiny took a turn that evening. Hiyam suddenly interrupted our laughter to say, "I've got it! You should take my old job." I was stunned. I protested that I had no experience, but that didn't seem to matter.

"Do you think I knew anything about being a secretary before I started? You'll figure it out!"

It sounded like the perfect escape, but my mother reacted angrily when I mentioned it. She insisted that I finish my degree before getting involved in anything else, but when she tried to enlist Ramzi's support, he was surprisingly supportive about the idea and stuck his neck out for me. "You should let her do it, Mama. All the students have jobs on the side."

My mother "let me" take the job, but she made me swear that I wouldn't neglect my studies no matter what. Neglecting my studies was the least of what was to come. Cigarette smoke and laughter hung in the air above Hiyam's bedroom that evening, above the beer bottle and strong cup of tea, and I decided I wanted to learn how to be carefree like Hiyam, if only just once. "Why don't you let me have a sip of your beer before I go back home?"

She didn't act surprised. Nothing about her reaction suggested that what I'd just said had been the least bit unexpected. When we first became friends, she constantly tried to get me to split a cold beer with her, but I always refused, and eventually she gave up.

This time, I was the one asking for a drink and acting far too nonchalant for a first-timer. After I drained the glass in a series of quick gulps, she went to fetch us another bottle. "We're out of lupini, but I'll get you some peanuts."

26

Why did I inherit my mother's hatred of alcohol? I didn't have a business to ruin like her father and my father's father. I didn't have any kids that I should have been sacrificing for—which was what she used to tell my father. It didn't make any sense. Why didn't I claim that other inheritance? The tradition of my ancestors who'd thrown it all away. A bequest of pleasure and self-indulgence. Knowing that you'll be in debt and ostracized forever; the villain of everyone's stories. But it's more than that. They'll always think of you the way I think of my father, and the way my parents thought of their fathers. They'll always make excuses for what the darkness made you do. With every failed romance, every insult, every new debt, someone who isn't like you gets to pity you. Even after they die, they get to stick around as part of your ongoing battle against the entire world. The conflict that gives you the motivation and strength to endure. You can be only one: Winner or loser, victim or bully, but there's no difference. They gave you life, and you took it from them, naively—like biting into a prickly pear in order to peel it. Those lonely, naked ancestors, who'd agreed to wear the costumes that others had chosen for them soon found they were never able to change out of them.

27

The next day, I went with Hiyam to meet the general manager, and as soon as the two of them had finished giggling at Hiyam's many witty quips, I had a new job. The general manager chose one of the other women to train me—the most experienced, most practical, and least attractive one of the bunch. She was also engaged to another colleague at the company. All the other women avoided me, thinking I was either trouble or uptight, but they smiled at me fakely and were encouraging as I learned to type on the Optima. As I started making more noise at my desk, the general manager would lean over affectionately as he walked by and congratulate me on being a quick study.

I was almost nineteen then and, in only a few months, I began to show signs of reneging on the deal I'd made with my mother. It was enough to make her insomniac for an entire month before my exams. I took all but the final two dutifully before my energy faded and ended up with a low pass and two re-takes.

The following morning, the general manager took me out in one of his fancy cars, which he always matched to the suit he was wearing. His over-the-top elegance concealed a scrawny figure and features that were almost monstrous. We went to meetings at all the big companies, where the employees welcomed him warmly, almost obsequiously, and on our way back, we stopped at a grand hotel, where we sat and chatted. He listened to me attentively as he drank two bottles of beer. He ordered me a fruit salad with ice cream because when he'd offered me a glass of beer, I'd rebuffed him, and he wanted to keep things civil.

He wasn't just a businessman who ran a large firm that looked like a beehive of activity when big deals were at stake. When he walked into a room, even the older employees leapt to their feet, and people would start to tremble if he ever raised his voice. He was a big deal. He consulted for all the biggest companies in Egypt, but what impressed me even more was that he had a doctorate in engineering from the UK. He'd worked as head engineer in a government agency before resigning to join the private sector in his fifties.

One of the new female employees tried to warn me about him. She'd got her job because of some distant family connection, but she didn't stay very long. She was beautiful—a wife and mother who genuinely loved her family, and she used to come to work every day in a fancy car like his. Her only problem was that she was bored at home, but after he took her for a pleasant chat at one of his favorite hotels, she quickly decided that she'd rather quit. "I can tell you have your eye on the doctor, but just be careful," she said to me in private shortly before she left. "He's married, and he's one of those guys who likes to use young women for fun. You're still very young, my dear, and I know you don't understand why I'm telling you this, but I feel like it's my duty." I was stunned. I'd tried so hard to conceal my true feelings, but she'd seen right through me. She didn't say anything else after that—simply gathered her things and walked out of the office. That was the last time I ever saw her.

28

A few weeks before my nineteenth birthday, Ramzi left a letter for me by my bedside so that I'd see it when I woke up. He would leave early in the morning and stay out all day, so we hardly saw each other at all. Perhaps I avoided him on purpose in order to spare us both a pointless conversation. His wife had spent the night at her parents' house, so I guessed he went to join her there because I didn't see him until the following evening, when the only words we exchanged were "Good night."

In the letter, he said that he wasn't sure what to think but that he felt sorry for me. I had confessed to my mother that I was madly in love with my boss and that he loved me back and wanted us to get married, so she, of course, went to Ramzi with news of the "catastrophe." Ramzi said that if I'd fallen in love with anyone else besides Dr. Mahmoud—with all due respect to him—he would have supported me without hesitation, and he tried, in his way, to console me: *Sometimes we fall in love with people who would be perfect for us if only the circumstances were different.* He admitted that he didn't know what was right in a situation like mine, so he had no choice—though it "pained" him—but to leave the decision up to our mother.

It goes without saying that Mama was completely against the marriage. She stayed awake all night trying to find a way to put an end to it. I could go abroad or quit my job, but the latter seemed a lot harder to execute. How could she get me to do something I didn't want to do, she wondered. For my part, I decided to turn the screw, so while she was thinking things over, I swallowed a whole pack of sedatives. When she came into my bedroom to announce the decision she'd reached, she found me unconscious and screamed. Ramzi came running, and the two of them took me to the family doctor—family secret-keeper—who saved my life.

Mahmoud and I got married in secret in the presence of a lawyer and two witnesses—Ramzi and Uncle Salem. It hadn't been easy, but the groom eventually persuaded Uncle Salem to attend to give the proceedings "gravitas"—his words. In return, Uncle Salem made him promise that we'd celebrate the marriage publicly as soon as he'd squared things with his wife. Even Tante Sharifa went along with the marriage. She usually tried to quash my impulses, but this time she was the one who'd done what she could to soften the blow for my mother. "There's no point fighting it, Suad. The more you try to stop it, the more she'll just cling to him. She's not a little girl anymore. We might not get to her in time if she tries to kill herself again. It's done now anyway. It could have been a lot worse."

I got my own marital bedroom in the house while we searched for "a fancy apartment," as my husband put it. Every time Ramzi or his wife passed by the bedroom, they jealously admired the white bedroom suite that had cost "hundreds of pounds." The bed was grand, and it had two built-in speakers that played music. Ramzi let me have the bedroom at the back because the fine, ornamented furniture wouldn't fit in any of the other rooms. In exchange, he got "an older brother," as he liked to say. Someone to listen to his problems and make them disappear. Even my mother came to view my husband as a member of the family over time. She would tell him what was on her mind, and he'd do his best to help her resolve the problem as best he could. If it weren't for my mother's constant nagging that he had to announce the marriage publicly, we'd have been a happy household for the first time in our lives.

29

Sometimes, I think I was punishing her for trying to kill herself when I was a child. When she told me that I couldn't have something I wanted, I'd dare her to rescue me from the jaws of death. I was the only one in the family who treated her like that. Even Ragi, who was perpetually depressed, had never tried to end his own life. He kept a photo of her brother who'd killed himself under the glass topper on his desk, like an icon, but he never once threatened to end his life. I'd opened her old wounds—the trauma of her brother's suicide—and mine—the trauma of her attempt. After she died, I only tried to end my life one other time, and it was sincere, it wasn't to manipulate anyone—I simply wanted to go—but I haven't tried again in the past twenty years.

All I asked for was a modest dower, a clinic for Ramzi, and a gold necklace with the words *God has willed it* inscribed on it. My mother was the one who insisted that I only ask for one necklace because she didn't want it to seem like we were cashing in. I couldn't wear a wedding ring because we didn't want our co-workers or neighbors to find out, so I wore a silver ring instead, which I inscribed—using a small nail—with both our names and the date we got married. We laughed together in our plush bed, he and I, as I discovered the pleasures of my body.

30

It was a small clinic in a working-class neighborhood—Imbaba, if I recall correctly—but a very nice one. My husband agreed to rent the space and furnish it on the condition that Ramzi gave me half of the monthly profits. I didn't care. I didn't even care about my own salary; I just took some of the money for cigarettes and gave the rest to my mother. Ramzi and I were so excited about the clinic that we tallied up the number of patients together at the end of each day. I used to visit him at the clinic and sit in the waiting room, watching it grow busier day by day and taking pride in the "hotshot" doctor's success. His wife had started working at a shop that sold exotic birds, and despite Ramzi's jealousy, he occasionally stood outside the shop to observe how she dealt with customers. He was proud of her "for getting her hands dirty," as he liked to say. He always praised her for helping out with the household expenses, paying for her own purchases, and being thrifty.

One evening after Ramzi's wife showed me all her new clothes and shoes, things I would have never dared buy for myself, I blew up at my mother and told her that I wanted to keep my salary just like Buthayna. I couldn't stand the look of utter sadness that overcame her, so I quickly took it back and kissed her forehead.

Ramzi still rebuked me for how I'd spoken to Mama. "She's getting older and she's frail now. If you'd spoken to her like that back in the day, she'd have slapped you. You're bullying her cause she's weak. It's disgraceful."

My mother was nearly sixty then. She'd had me right before she turned forty and my father turned fifty.

They had me late—or by mistake, as my mother liked to say in jest. Toward the end of her life, when she was laid up sick in bed, I used to tell her: "That mistake you made turned out to be the best thing you ever did." She'd smile sweetly and begin singing and swaying in bed:

When I heard, "It's a boy!"
My heart filled with joy.

31

Ramzi sold the clinic, but I didn't hear about it until much later when my husband found out. He flew into a rage and accused me of "deceiving him" because I'd led him to believe that Ramzi had been giving me my share of the profits for months. He didn't confront Ramzi, however, because he knew that would mean that he'd have to live up to his end of the bargain and tell people that we were married. Ramzi and his wife had just welcomed their first child, a girl, so my husband chose not to disturb the elation and new life-rhythm that had taken root in our home. He was worried that I'd want a baby of my own, and the happiness I'd felt when my niece was born was keeping him up at night. It kept me up at night, too.

"If you had a kid, you'd understand," Ramzi told me as he tried to justify selling the clinic without my knowledge. When I began to sob, he didn't know how to staunch the unforeseen wound. It hadn't occurred to him that something like that would upset me. He kept apologizing and holding me tightly until I stopped crying. "She's mine, too, you know?" I said as I tickled the baby. "Don't people say that aunts are another mother?"

32

It wasn't the first time I'd been told not to bully my mother when she was vulnerable. When I was thirteen years old, my father slapped me for the first and only time—it was historic. My mother was laid up in bed with a herniated disc, and the pain was so bad it made her scream. She'd asked me to do something—I can't even remember what it was now. I guess I refused and was quite rude about it, so my father walked up to me very calmly and almost knocked me off my feet with a slap that made my ears ring. He'd never hit me before, so I hadn't seen it coming. I started bawling and quickly withdrew to the nearest wall, but Ramzi lost his shit. "You have no right to hit her! I'm not going to let you do that!" He shouted.

"She needs to learn not to speak to her mother like that ever again."

My father didn't so much as intervene again after that, except for one time when Ramzi cursed me for some forgotten reason. "I'm still here," he shouted. "After I'm dead, you can treat your sister like crap, but so long as I'm alive, I'm not going to allow it. Do you understand me?"

Mama was the only person who used to hit me. I learned to dodge the slippers flying through the air, but if she got her hands on me, she'd beat me viciously before insisting through tears that we make up. Once when I was fourteen, she started hitting me, and rather than scream and try to run away like I usually did, I just locked eyes with her. I don't know what it was about my look that frightened her, but her hands froze in the air and she started to tremble and shout, "Why are you looking at me like that? Huh? Why are you looking at me like that?" That was the last time she ever hit me.

33

An awful quarrel, separation, heartbreak! No matter what he did, I would never take him back. With my high school diploma in hand, I applied for a job at a German airline, and during the interview, I informed the German manager that I'd spent a few months in his country. That may have triggered his homesickness because he put the sheet with the interview questions on it to one side, to the consternation of his colleagues, and we just had a friendly chat. I'd spoken to some people who were interviewed before me, and they complained that the manager was "dry" and "pretentious." At first, I was a bit uncomfortable making small talk because I was worried that we'd get on to the topic of my trip to Germany and he'd somehow get me to admit that I'd violated the conditions of my visa, but he didn't seem very interested in the details of my stay. He wanted to know if I spoke German, so I told him, "I can understand a lot, but my speaking skills are very limited," which was the truth. He asked me about my hobbies. "Writing, reading, and poetry." I could see the interpreter was smiling, but she was facing the other direction, as though to say *I'm not here*. He asked me to name a book that I loved, so I said the first thing that came into my head: "Charles Dickens." We talked about Dickens, Goethe, and Baudelaire as well as my obsession with Tennessee Williams.

"What about music?"

"Bach, of course. And Mozart."

He seemed very happy and quite bemused. Despite my poor English, which I was trying to squeeze into the conversation as much as I could, and my elementary German, he accepted me in the program on the spot. I'd embarked on the journey of becoming a flight attendant, and the whole family was happy for me—even Buthayna, who lent me some of her fashionable outfits for the training course I had to attend.

Everything I'd said in the interview was true. Ragi had always made sure that I had books to read. As soon as I finished one, he'd give me another, and by the time I was fifteen, I'd read the Russian, French, German, and English classics and had also been made to listen to the grand symphonies. I hated most of them, but I fell forever in love with Emily Brontë and Françoise Sagan. Mozart I could tolerate, but Beethoven, to me, was tedious and irksome.

I didn't know how else to get Ragi to pay attention to me or how to interact with him without complication and strife. He was at his best when he was giving me a book or trapping me in his bedroom to make me listen to a record, and nothing made him happier than when I reported back to him about what I'd enjoyed or disliked about a particular book. He was determined to help me understand anything I'd found obscure.

I spent my whole life praising him for the impact he had on me. Whenever anyone asked me about the books I read as a child, I proudly acknowledged the role played by my eldest brother. He was the one who'd laid the foundations. If it hadn't been for him, I never would have become a writer because I pretty much stopped reading as soon as he went abroad.

When he returned to Egypt after having lived in Germany for more than thirty years, I reminded him of the all-important role that he'd played and told him how grateful I was for everything that he'd done. An attempt to establish a dialogue based on our shared past. He appeared taken aback as though I'd imagined the whole thing. As an adult, I'd spent my entire life reading and writing, but Ragi mocked me for it. He was clueless about literature; he'd stopped reading and forgotten everything he'd read. It was as though he'd left all that behind him in his childhood bedroom. He tried to introduce me to his new world by playing some techno, which young people like, but I couldn't stand it. Who was this stranger? All my memories felt like fabulations.

34

For the dream of a different life, I summoned the diligent student of my past. A cup of coffee, a packet of cigarettes, an English-language book about aviation, and an Arabic-English dictionary on the table in front of me. My keys to success. As I deciphered the code and took notes, my mother would cheer me on whenever she walked past and an upbeat Ramzi would pat me on the back.

Mornings, I woke up as soon as the birds started chirping, gathered my things, and headed to class, and once there, I answered the questions more quickly and more precisely than any of my classmates. During our breaks and the splendid meals they fed us, I was happy to explain topics to my classmates that they'd failed to understand. Onboard the aircraft for training, I looked out of the window at the horizon. Soon, the trips would start and I'd travel the world.

Traveling the world had a special ring to it. The fancy hotels where I'd be staying—this time without my husband—had an aura of temptation and misgiving. The elegantly perfumed flight attendants laughed without shame, and they were at ease with the rest of the crew, especially with the purser, whom I found repulsive. The first time he met me, he smiled and said, "Finally, someone listened to me. I've been telling them to send us more pretty girls." Everything that took place around me felt like it was behind a pane of glass, like the windows of the airplane that was going to show me the world.

There was one week of classes left before the final exam, and I was pushing myself as though it was the last chance I'd ever get. Outside in the street, my sweetheart honked his horn, so I ran out—pulse racing—and found him, pouting in his car, safe from any run-ins with Ramzi or our mother. He'd disappeared after arguments in the past, but rarely for more than a couple of days. This time he'd been gone more than two months. My heart ached the entire time. I'd never wanted to become a flight attendant, not even as a child. After all, it was quite similar to the receptionist jobs that my cousins had, which I'd felt were beneath me. But it was a safe way out, financially safe at least. I could see Mama and Ramzi's eyes glaze over when I told them about our visit to the catering division, which had smelled awful and made me nauseated. They took us there so we could get a feel for every aspect of the operation. On the way there, we were packed into the back of a truck, which was humiliating because every time the truck moved, I crashed into my co-workers. They even stopped suddenly to give us a taste of turbulence. I complained about my male co-workers' lame attempts to hit on me, too, but my complaints were pretty minor. Too minor to make someone give up a good job like that one. Too minor even by my own standards because the only other thing I could do—after the romance had burned out—was to go back to university.

There he was on my street, and there we were having dinner at the restaurant where we'd had our first date. We talked through our problems, and then he said, "No wife of mine is going to work as a flight attendant," to which I acquiesced because the sound of the word "wife" had enchanted me. It felt like the long-delayed promise would finally be fulfilled: a life together! I promised him that I'd go back to working at his company, and on our way out, we nearly floated through the doors we were so happy.

When my mother heard the news, she grumbled a bit, although not for very long. Ramzi, on the other hand, tore the house apart when I told him. He'd never done anything like that before, so it took us all by surprise. I sheltered by a wall as he threw whatever he could at me. My mother was in shock, but when he began to kick me, she moved her body between us. "I'm never going to let you out of the house again! You've disgraced us all!" Ramzi shouted. He eventually calmed down a bit and went into his bedroom, but Mama and I waited until we were certain that he'd fallen asleep before we climbed out through the balcony at dawn and took shelter at my old nanny Auntie Saadeya's house. I called my husband to tell him what had happened, so he went to speak to Ramzi, and later I found out that Ramzi pulled a knife on him and said, "If you don't make the marriage public, I swear I'm going to kill you." We set a date, and my husband told me that I should go back to the house in the meanwhile because Ramzi wasn't well. Mama and I were very anxious when we arrived, but as soon as he opened the door, Ramzi embraced us both tightly, like a child who thought he'd been lost. He cried hysterically, but we managed to soothe him.

35

When the old friend who lived in Germany came back home for a visit, he persuaded Ramzi to return to Germany with him so that he could help set him up out there. He told Ramzi he could stay at his house while he worked at a hospital and learned German. "You have nothing to lose. I'll cover your expenses, and if it doesn't work out, you'll at least have gone on a trip."

Although we'd completely lost contact with Ragi, as though the earth had swallowed him up, my mother wasn't worried about the scenario repeating. Ramzi was already a physician, and he'd be taking his wife and child with him. But she did make him swear on her life that he'd go look for his older brother.

They stayed with our family friend and his German wife for a few months, and the couple treated Ramzi and

Buthayna's daughter like she was their own, showering her with affection and gifts. The wife was too old to have kids, and our family friend was infertile, too. He just kept it a secret from his wife because he wanted to play the part of the virile young man.

As time went on, all of Ramzi's attempts to find a job came to naught, and his dream of working as a doctor in Germany with nothing more than a bachelor's in medicine began to fade. He wasn't prepared to give up on his career, so he moved his family back to Egypt. All they had to show for their time was a gift of dollars from our family friend that would cover their expenses while Ramzi looked for a job, including some new clothes for his wife and daughter.

To avoid any repeat of the knife incident and to make good on my husband's promise, we went to see the sheikh while Ramzi and his family were in Germany. I wore an ordinary summer dress, and my husband, who was usually in an elegant suit, put on a dress shirt and slacks. My mother didn't accompany us—out of dejection, I guess—so we hired a couple of witnesses and made our marriage official. We went to a hotel cafe afterward, but when we got there, my husband started to panic. He couldn't stop worrying about how his first wife would react when she received a copy of the marriage certificate, which was how the law worked back then. He started imagining what people would say:

"He married a girl the same age as his daughter."

"After a lifetime together."

"She'll make him pay. He'll never see his kids again."

He was somewhere else, having an entire conversation with himself, as I sat there, heavy-hearted, nursing my beer—the drink he'd introduced me to.

36

The office wasn't a happy place in those days. He'd been overconfident and stubborn while trying to monopolize the market for a certain piece of equipment, so the big boys went after him where he was most vulnerable, and he was forced to sell off his entire stock as scrap. He'd poured his entire fortune into it, so he was broke, and he had to let most of the employees go. He did manage to hold on to two of his sportscars, which he took when he went around to different companies to try to save his business. The only staff left were me and the kind-hearted, elderly accountant, who'd been my husband's loyal companion from the very beginning.

When Ramzi and his family got back from Germany, he was happy to hear that we'd registered the marriage. I'd told him about it over the phone, but he'd insisted "on seeing it with his own eyes." My husband was broke, but he still had his reputation, so he went off to Libya to consult for one of the big oil companies there a few days before Ramzi and his family returned from Germany. It was the perfect escape. An escape from debt and his first wife. I jumped every time the doorbell rang after he left, expecting her to turn up with her parents and kids to rough me up or cause a scene, but she never did. She bore the crisis with silent contempt. I later learned that she considered it to be "their issue" and that "the girl" wasn't part of the equation. For months, my husband sent letters with diminishing frequency until eventually they stopped coming. That was back in the early 80s and Libya had already cut off relations with Egypt because of the Camp David Accords. He'd said he'd send me a visa so that I could go join him there, so when I opened the envelope, my heart was pounding and my hands trembled, but the post had been delayed, and the visa was no longer valid. I would later discover that it had been forged on a typewriter and post-dated. I would also learn that his first wife had gone to visit him there with their two kids during the summer break; that was the "delay" in my visa. We met in another Arab country not long after that and that was when he told me, after much arguing, that he'd decided not to divorce his first wife because he didn't want to disrupt their children's lives. That precipitated a much bigger argument during which I accused him of going back on all the promises he'd made about starting a life together. He offered me an alternative: we could meet periodically in different countries to see the sights and spend time together, but at the end of the trip, each of us would return to our respective houses. Naturally, I refused. He did exactly as he'd threatened to do—"If you don't go along with it, I'll just leave you hanging"—and disappeared. For the next three years. Eventually, the court ruled that he was absent and abusive, and for the first time in my life, I was handed divorce papers. I took them into my bedroom and shut the door so that I could be alone with them, and no matter how hard my mother knocked because she could hear me sobbing, I didn't open it again until the following morning.

37

Ramzi and his family stayed with us for a few months after they returned from Germany. After completing his internship, he'd vowed that he'd never work in a government hospital "even if it meant begging in the street," as he so often said. He felt his destiny lay elsewhere. When he got offered a job in Saudi Arabia, we were all elated.

Ramzi went there on his own at first so that he could find a suitable apartment for his young family, who went to stay with his in-laws as they usually did when he went away. He used to call his wife every day to tell her how much he missed her, but he wasn't allowed to return home at all during the three-month probation period. They cried together over the phone, but whenever he suggested quitting and coming back, Buthayna stood firm.

In the two months that Ramzi spent weeping like an orphan, he only sent a letter or two back home to Mama and me, so I was surprised to hear his voice on the other end when the phone rang one night. He begged me to send him a telegram saying that our mother was gravely ill and wanted to see him one last time before she died. It was a silly scheme because our mother was in perfectly good health, and I also thought it was poor judgment to tempt fate like that. My mother took pity on him, however. "Do you really think we have any say about when somebody dies? It's all up to God," she said in an attempt to assuage me. I pitied him, too, to be honest.

"I swear that son of yours won't stop lying until he's dead."

"God forbid! Take me first, Lord!"

I sent the telegram, and apparently Ramzi's Saudi sponsor also took pity on him because he gave him a few days of leave to go see his mother one last time. He went straight from the airport to the shop where his wife worked, and stood outside on the sidewalk watching her until she noticed him and ran out. They embraced in the street in front of all the passers-by, they told us when they came over to the house, giggling.

It's only recently that I've learned that there are two things that you should never joke about: illness and death. When you mention them, the ears in the ether prick up. Illness and death fail to recognize innuendo, metaphor, and white lies. They take the things we say literally; they do exactly as they're told. You'd have to be an idiot to think that all our destinies are laid out in full. We issue instructions when we're not thinking and then quickly forget about them, but their fulfillment, when it comes, is always sudden and unerring.

38

My grandfather died two years before his son. My mother was sad, but my father didn't appear to be. I cried a lot, and I continued to miss my grandfather's bedroom for a long while after. I used to sit with him in there while he made me listen to magnificent poems and claim that he was the one who wrote them. I once recited the first two lines of "You're Holding Back Tears" to my friends at elementary school, and after receiving their applause, announced that my grandfather was the author. The Arabic teacher had overheard, so he told me to "stop telling lies." I was so angry that I didn't sleep a wink that night, and the following morning, I informed my mother that I wouldn't be going to school. She affirmed my decision earnestly because she wanted to validate my feelings, but she could barely keep a straight face. I wasn't aware of it at the time, but she'd already spoken to the teacher and explained that I'd had no idea that I wasn't telling the truth.

I forced Mama to take me to see my grandfather first thing in the morning so that I could confront him. I wanted to make him pay for humiliating me in front of my friends and our teacher, but he didn't so much as blink. He just stared at me.

"Your teacher's an idiot."

"Even Mama said that someone called Abu Firas wrote it! You lied to me."

He chose not to take offense. "Oh, your mother—," he said, waving his hand in the air. "What does she know about anything?"

I have no idea how we made up after that, but we soon went back to sitting together in his room like nothing had ever happened.

My grandmother died not long after he did as though he'd been a placenta connecting her to vitality. She lost weight, got sick, grew depressed, and died. It was a quick decline. My mother and father both grieved her, and a kind of compassion grew between them as between a mother and an orphan. By the time aunt Ihsan died, my father had already been dead for years, but I'm certain he would have been as sad as the rest of us. The door to the house near the El-Sayyida Aisha Mosque was closed to me forever after that.

My uncle's children continued living there for years, except for the youngest, whom I've never even met. I loved them, but I couldn't help but feel they were relatives once-removed, and even when I used to see them on occasion when I went to visit my aunt, they still kept their distance. The only exception was my male cousin, who used to bring me a big chocolate bar when he came to the movies with me and my mother. He'd left education after graduating with a technical diploma, and even though my mother really liked him, she couldn't tolerate Aunt Ihsan's hints, which started when I entered middle school, that the two of us would get married. My mother stopped taking us out together and my aunt, who loved her nephew like a son, took offense. She hadn't expected snobbery from my mother.

Eventually, they both got over it.

Strangers Playing Ping-Pong

1

He blew up at us while we were sitting in his flashy car and caused such a commotion that the people driving past turned to look. My mother was sitting beside him in the passenger seat, and I was in the back. Me, Ramzi, Mama. It was rare for the three of us to be alone together without his wife. My mother had expressed her doubts about the diagnosis of the doctor we'd just visited, and I'd agreed. Ramzi started out calmly, saying that the doctor was an old friend and the leader in his field, but when my mother started asking questions and saying "Oh, I don't know about that," he exploded. He told her that she'd tormented Ragi and him as children when she'd had renal colic. Claimed that she'd abandoned him as though he wasn't even her son—something she'd never done to Ragi or me. It was like he was reciting from a bitter book he'd memorized cover-to-cover. One gripe after the other, in sequence, without pause. "No one has ever stood by me except for my wife," was the stirring conclusion. He got us both with that one. As I watched Mama deflating in her seat, head in her hands, I tried to stand up for her.

"No one was ever there for you? Is that right?"

He turned his entire body to look at me. "Yeah, I know. A long time ago, your mother and me sold you off to that doctor. Are you happy now?" I swallowed the insulting description of my first love because I knew in that moment that no matter how I struck back, the woman sitting beside him would pay the heavy price. Silence.

We happened to drive by our old house in Nasr City that night. It flashed by in a blur as I cried in the back seat of Ramzi's fast, angry car. I couldn't stop crying, but my mother's face had turned to stone and she was just staring out at the road and the cars passing by. When I reached out to grab her shoulder, she didn't squeeze my hand like she always did. When Ramzi looked back in the rear-view mirror, I saw a tear in his eye, and after we'd pulled up at the house, he gave me a tight hug. He tried to hug Mama, too, but she dodged him and said that she wanted to be alone for the rest of the night.

2

Someone somewhere in the wide-open sky batted a ping-pong ball into the air and it landed on Mama's chest one night when she was sixty-seven. It sat on top of her rib cage between her slack breasts, and occasionally when it would hurt her, she'd rub it back into place. Everyone reassured her and explained that it was a good sign that it was firm and unmovable because tumors were usually squishy, and you can move them along with your finger. Ramzi's doctor friend had told her that it was rheumatoid arthritis.

Mama applied ointment every night and, having learned her lesson, never expressed any reservations. It helped that the pain wasn't very intense.

She'd had two operations already. Ramzi, who was working abroad, had sent us enough money to cover both—including hospital fees and medications—plus he got a discount for being in the doctors' union and his surgeon friend and the anesthesiologist both did him a solid and waived their fee.

In the first operation, they had removed a tumor the size of a small fetus from Mama's neck because she could hardly breathe. I stared at the tumor floating in preservation fluid as though it were a baby in an incubator. One of my friends who's a doctor had accompanied me to the hospital that morning, and she reacted as soon as she noticed me trembling hysterically, injecting me with a sedative that went to work right away as I stroked my mother to wake her up from the anesthetic.

For years, Mama was under the care of a famous and elderly doctor, and she dutifully took her thyroid medicine each morning. She was just happy that it was cheap and easy to get. As her health began to deteriorate, her doctor died, so she went to see our family doctor—the one who'd treated my father. "Do I really have to take this medicine for the rest of my life?" She asked him.

"Yes, for the rest of your life. If you stop, you'll drop dead." She never forgave the man for his "churlish" answer, and for days after that, I could hear her talking to herself in anger, vowing to get back at him, but she calmed down eventually. She decided to pretend that the incident had never happened and to stick to her old doctor's instructions. "The one who used to be Abdel Nasser's doctor. Not that other jerk." She stopped going to the doctor after that, and over time, her neck swelled up little by little until one night she could barely breathe, so I rushed her to the nearest hospital.

3

At twenty-six, I couldn't imagine what life would be like after my mother died. Years before, I'd switched my degree from psychology to business so that I could help my husband—the PhD in engineering—run his firm. It was a bad decision and the justification for it evaporated after the divorce. The textbooks all looked like a bunch of mathematical formulas. One time, my mother tried to help me study by offering to read my economics textbooks to me out loud. "This is easy!" she insisted. "Even I get it." She also begged one of the neighbors to give me accounting lessons for free. After two very strange years, I passed all my exams but two, and by some miracle, I managed to graduate. I promptly began writing poetry.

The black sheep's here. The black sheep's gone out. The black sheep confronts death all by herself.

4

When we got the biopsy results back, we celebrated, and my mother passed refreshments out to the neighbors, while leaning on me to avoid putting pressure on the wound. We were told that a rare fungus had spread inside my mother's thyroid, and her history with rare illnesses like tapeworm lent the diagnosis credibility. Ramzi vouched for it, too, when he spoke to Mama on the phone. He'd called his friend, of course, to thank him for taking care of his mother, and then called him a second time to congratulate him on his promotion, much of which rested on the discovery of the rare fungus.

I could never escape fear's grip after that, though. "What will I do if Mama dies?"

I could have never imagined falling in love with him the first time we met. He was nice, though. An artist who seemed like he'd had some adventures but was ready to settle down. After he came over to the house to ask my mother for permission to marry me, she tried to warn me. "He's uncouth. I don't like him at all." I wrote poems, and he wrote film scripts and plays. I used to think that artists could live like that.

When I called Ramzi to tell him that I was planning to get married, he asked me to wait until his next visit during the summer holidays. "He can't take a few days off for his sister's wedding? I guess it isn't that important to him," was my boyfriend's response. My body wanted it and my nerves made me want it more, so we went to the sheikh and got married and then returned back home in high spirits to Mama, who was lying in bed recuperating from her operation. She offered faint congratulations. My new husband's apartment was still under construction, and I was completely sincere about staying by my mother's side during her illness, so he moved in with us into our rented apartment in Heliopolis, where a new family took shape.

5

Ramzi took the news of my marriage and my new husband moving in with suppressed anger. He didn't call or send a letter after we got married, and he and his family spent the summer holidays at his in-laws' house because he still hadn't saved up enough to buy an apartment. The couple had just welcomed another daughter. Ramzi and his wife came over for a simple dinner that my husband had prepared, and while Ramzi didn't take to him, he did tell him to look after me.

He rarely came over to visit our mother, so she mostly went to see him at his in-laws', and I'm sure she spent the whole time complaining to him about the "lunatic" her daughter had moved into the house. She had every right, too; the battle between the two of them was well underway. First, he kicked her out of the kitchen because he enjoyed cooking, and then he'd only cook dishes that she disliked or that inflamed her chest allergy before bed. She begged him to stop through a constant cough, but he just ignored her.

I didn't believe her when she told me that she was going to bed hungry because he used to put the food on the top shelf, where she couldn't reach it. I thought she was playing the role of spiteful mother-in-law until I saw him do it one night with my own two eyes.

The conflict between the two of us flourished in silence, as we lay in bed and gathered with friends. I chose to overlook his affronts, even those against my mother, and she did her best to keep out of it, as well. Until she couldn't restrain herself. In the middle of a violent argument, I'd called out to her, "Mama, come help me," so she thrust herself between the two of us. He was so frightened of her that he made himself scarce for a couple of days.

Ramzi turned up at the house immediately after receiving my mother's call like he was the emergency services. I was lying in bed after my husband had attacked me, when Ramzi and his wife walked in. "I can't be married to a man who hits me."

"Don't forget this is your second marriage. You don't get another chance." His wife shot him an angry look, but I was surprised to find him sounding calm and rational. To me, it felt like he was being honest and empathetic. He was a lifeline.

"Why shouldn't she get a divorce?" his wife asked. "I know people who've been divorced three or four times!"

My mother remained neutral—an uncommon occurrence; she even left the room while I was speaking to Ramzi and Buthayna. Ramzi had criticized her for getting involved in my marriage so many times that she decided to leave us alone to talk. It's true that Buthayna was in the room with us, but Mama believed that my brother and I shared a secret connection, and perhaps she was right. Or maybe she was scared—as I was—that she would soon be dead, and she just wanted to see the world as it would be after she was gone.

When Ramzi and his wife flew back to Saudi Arabia a few days later, my mother did her best to be kind, and I did my best to move past what had happened, but the derangement gradually resurfaced. That's how it ended. Knives brandished inches from my face. Neighbors watching from their balconies as he chased me in the street, listening to glass break over and over again in our quiet house, our uncommonly quiet home of thirty years. Amidst all the tall buildings, ours was a single story, and no one had ever heard us make a peep. He wanted money in exchange for a divorce, but Ramzi refused to pay him, so I had to turn to my friend Ra'ifa's husband, who took care of everything.

6

But then suddenly it didn't matter whether my mother knocked or I shut the bedroom door. After hiding out at Ra'ifa's house for a while, I came back home to find all the doors open and the house stripped bare. He'd even prized the light switches off the walls. Wires poked out of the cavity like torn intestines. When I walked into my bedroom and saw all my clothes in shreds on the floor, I began slapping myself on the face over and over. I was still slapping myself hard when I heard my mother saying, "Good riddance!" but as soon as she realized what I was doing, she ran over and grabbed my hand. We arm wrestled until I finally regained my senses.

7

Ramzi came around to the idea that divorce had been my only option after I told him that my ex-husband was continuing to make threats. He used to bang on our door in the middle of the night, drunk, trying to break in. It was humiliating. I told Ramzi I was so afraid that I was considering paying a thug to stand outside our building for a few days. I needed Ramzi to give me some money if I was going to be able to do that, but he didn't want to get involved. "Let's talk about it the next time we see each other. I understand what you're going through. I swear if he tries to do anything to me or my wife and kids, I'll teach him a lesson." There was no way I could miss it. He'd listed exactly who he was going to protect. We were two separate families, I realized as I listened to him speak. The links had come apart and I would have to face my battles on my own.

Mama and I threw ourselves into fixing up the house and removing any signs of past altercations. She was excited, happy to have survived it, and a bit wary that I might get back with him. That romance might lure me back to the "lunatic." I didn't let it, though, and she eventually relaxed. We changed the locks and bought a heavy metal padlock for extra security when we went out, and we never opened the door without looking through the peephole first.

We borrowed a small mattress from our kindhearted neighbor to put on my grandmother's daybed, which was the only thing that the lunatic hadn't destroyed or carried off—that and the elegant wooden set from Assiut, which we'd also inherited from my grandmother. Our neighbor had an iron gate installed, and she kept both the gate and her front door shut when she was at home with her husband and children because she was afraid that the frenzy might spread. Either because my ex-husband would want to get back at her for helping us or because he wanted to use her to get to me. After several intense months, my mother and I finally slept soundly, side by side.

The crisis had passed. Like all crises do. When my mother wrote to Ramzi asking him to send money so that she could buy some furniture on installment, he wrote back immediately and said that we should send a list (complete with prices) of everything that we needed and that he'd send the money straightaway. We spent days writing out lists and carefully going over them, crossing out anything that seemed like a luxury because we didn't want to overburden him, but before we'd even sent our modest final list, he called and informed us cheerfully that he was coming for a visit.

8

They covered the entire floor of the apartment with blue vinyl, so we could no longer see the tiles underneath. Once when my mother and I were alone together, she confessed to me that she hated it, and I agreed. The old tiles were beautiful; each had its own unique pattern of geometric or floral designs. They'd faded because of the cleaning products my mother so often used, but we still recognized them.

The blue was dark, like a bruise. We knew where it had come from, too, and that made it worse: a factory owned by Buthayna's uncle. "This is so fashionable," she said once the vinyl had dried. "All my uncle's kids have had it done, and he gave us a big discount on it."

I was happy to move back into the bedroom at the back. At some points, I had to avoid looking at the other bedroom on my way to the bathroom because I was worried that I'd be overwhelmed by difficult memories. The furniture in the cramped sitting room was made of fine wood and upholstered in a brown floral print velour. The dining table could seat six, but we had to remove the leaf so it would fit. There was a new tv and video player and a new refrigerator and stove, both a good size. In my bedroom, there was a new single bed and a small wardrobe. Mama chose to sleep on the daybed she'd inherited from her mother, so Ramzi bought her a new mattress. She returned the one that we'd borrowed to our neighbor with customary gratitude, but she kept the woman's 14-inch, black-and-white, orange-backed Toshiba television, which she had to tip from side to side to get the picture right. "Why are you so attached to that thing?" he asked her.

"It has my shows, and that's all I care about."

Ramzi nodded and then promptly moved the new color television into his own bedroom. The furniture from Assiut was out, too. Buthayna told Mama that it didn't go with the new furniture that she and Ramzi had bought and there was no room for it, so we decided to split it up. I took two chairs and the table to work on plus an extra chair for my guests. I also moved my father's clothes stand into my room. Mama crammed the sofa and the remaining two chairs into her tiny bedroom.

None of it came as a surprise. As soon as he'd arrived, Ramzi sat Mama, Buthayna, and me down together for a "candid conversation." He told us that he couldn't afford to furnish our apartment as well as his own, so he and Buthayna had decided to move in with us and we just had to make the best of it. I felt too guilty to risk saying anything, and my mother, who was obviously unhappy, seemed to have also decided that the only thing she could do was agree. She welcomed them. Anything for family.

9

Buthayna was always mocking our family—and not just our small nucleus either—and Ramzi always seemed to find it funny. Mama and I would have gladly joined in on the laughter if she didn't always pick on such strange things. Like when she said it was "so unlikely" that a family like ours had produced PhDs. My mother and I couldn't understand why that made Ramzi laugh. He only had a BA in medicine, while some of his colleagues had earned doctorates, but his main priority was making money. In the past, he might have envied those colleagues, but now he agreed with Buthayna wholeheartedly. In my head, I answered every one of her snide remarks with one of my own—but only in my head. Mama couldn't stand it. It reminded her of something that Buthayna had told her when Ramzi was in the final-year of medical school. "You know, I don't really care if he passes or not."

"As the one who raised him, I do care."

Buthayna's criticisms got on my mother's nerves because they probably reminded her of those difficult years when she'd had to push Ramzi to finish his degree and shoulder some of the responsibility.

He did get rich in the end, as he liked to say. He specialized in dermatology and began making creams for hair and skin. He once boasted to me about how much he got paid to massage old men's testicles in Saudi

Arabia, and then asked where he could buy plastic jars in bulk for his products.

10

Buthayna's parents hailed from a small village near Mit Ghamr, and her father had enlisted in the army as a young man. Her mother was left with an intellectual disability as a result of an untreated thyroid condition as a child, so her brother had decided to marry her off to the soldier who was five years her junior. God was good to that brother, and he did well in the ceramic tile business, which was just starting in the seventies—well enough to build a factory. He also bought some land on the outskirts of town—or Nozha, to you and me—where he built an apartment building. He and his family occupied the first floor. When the soldier, by then a first lieutenant, was nearly fifty, he came down with tuberculosis and had to retire, so he was made a major in recognition of his long career and his wife's brother invited him and his family to move into one of the other apartments. He wanted his sister to have the upper hand in her marriage because her husband so often condescended to her.

Buthayna's family was the inverse of ours: a second daughter followed a few years after the first one, but eventually they had a baby boy, their little prince.

Buthayna's uncle truly loved his sister so he provided for her and her family, but that meant that he got to boss everyone around. He was even snide to Ramzi when he went over to meet his future in-laws and ask for permission to marry their daughter. His children never treated their cousins with much consideration, and Buthayna was genuinely hurt by the way they lorded everything over her: their fancy private schools, trendy clothes, and cars—one for each cousin parked end to end out in front of the building. The cousins loved one another, of course, but they weren't as close as siblings. Their father hadn't passed that kind of affection down to them, or maybe he had, but benefactors couldn't help being smug.

Despite the old hurt, Buthayna always boasted about her uncle and his family, and Ramzi, for his part, also paid them a lot of respect and did what he could to keep them happy. Although he'd learned some arrogance from his in-laws, Ramzi was always kind to Buthayna's uncle, and every time the couple came back to Egypt on vacation, they'd update him about how much money they'd made until eventually the two families were more or less equally well off. At that point, the relationship between them fizzled some, and Ramzi even let it be known from time to time that he wasn't happy with the way Buthayna's uncle and his family spoke to him and his daughters. Buthayna no longer envied her cousin's stylish outfits, and she rarely dressed up herself any more. She would only bring out the gold and diamonds for special occasions. She'd gained weight, so she appeared slightly rotund in her roomy dresses and headscarf, and her dark black hair was always hidden away, except for a single lock that hung over her forehead. She tried to pretend it was an accident whenever Ramzi told her to tuck it back in.

11

I'm not sure if my mother was exaggerating when she said that she'd had to walk all the way back to Heliopolis from

Dokki after receiving a lecture from her sister about her wasteful spending. My aunt had refused to lend Mama any money and wouldn't even give her enough for a bus ticket home. When I was a child, I fully believed her version of events because I'd seen her walk through the door, tearful and exhausted. I had also been forced to spend a week at my aunt's house, so I could imagine what she'd been through. When I was very young, perhaps not even seven, my mother had sent me to stay at my aunt's house, so that I wouldn't catch measles from my brothers back home in Alf Maskan. She gave me a generous amount of pocket money—three times as much as I usually got—so that it would last me for two weeks, and she spent the whole trip listing the many pleasures that awaited me: I could get sugar-cane juice on the corner and roasted seeds and peanuts just a few meters away. My aunt's husband was "just the sweetest." He was a tough and stern teacher, but he left that side of him at school. At home, he was calm and meek, taking direction from his wife, who was far sterner than he was. Their daughter, who was eight years older than me, the same age as Ramzi, treated me like a younger sister, but their two sons were much older. Both were in the College of Engineering, where one worked as a teaching assistant and the other was still finishing his undergraduate degree. They horsed around with me in passing, and the oldest, who was a very competent pianist, occasionally tried to teach me how to play, but when I started producing discordant noise, he'd laugh and gently push me away.

As soon as I got to my aunt's house, I handed over the money my mother gave me for safekeeping. I wanted her to see that I was being disciplined. I asked my aunt to give me just enough money for a jug of sugar-cane juice and two packets of roasted seeds and peanuts each day, but she didn't. Instead, I got humorless speeches about being irresponsible just like my mother. At seven each evening, she'd escort me into her bedroom, where she'd laid a small mattress out for me, and expect me to go to sleep right away because that was what children were supposed to do.

Of course, I did have some fun when I was staying with them. There was a garden at the back where I was allowed to pick green apples. My aunt didn't mind if I picked them, but only after she'd taught me how to tell when they were ripe. The mango tree was a different story. If I so much as went near it, she'd bolt to her feet and collect as many of the small green fruits as she could before wrapping them carefully in newspaper.

Her husband was kind to me. He introduced me to the rabbits in the hutch by name, and always made sure that I was distracted elsewhere so that I wouldn't see him slaughtering one of the chickens.

My aunt didn't let me use the telephone, which had a coinbox attached to it, so I couldn't tell my mother about the hell she was putting me through. About the enforced bedtimes while everyone else watched television, about the fight that I'd had with my aunt: "I gave you my money, and now you won't give it back. You're a thief!" I couldn't tell her that my aunt insisted on handing me a broom and dustpan each morning so that I could sweep the area in front of the large window, which overlooked the main road, until it sparkled. She used to run her finger over the window frame to inspect my work before she'd let me have any of my own money. If I hadn't seen the way she abused the young maid—who wasn't much older than me and who'd come straight from the countryside in a tattered dress and a scarf covering her shaved head—I would have guessed that she thought of me as a servant.

As fate would have it, one day my cousin insisted on taking me with her to visit a friend despite my aunt's objection, and there, I was able to find a telephone and call my mother. Despite all the sobbing, she understood what I was saying and she promised that she'd come to get me the next day. I continued to sob because I was worried that she might change her mind, but she assured me that she wouldn't. By the time we got back to my aunt's house, Dad was already there because, as my mother later explained, he wasn't going to let me stay there for another moment once he'd heard how I was being treated. He had just come home from teaching when my mother told him. "Why should I wait until the morning? I'm going to go get her now!" On the way back home, I floated on air. He bought me as many chocolates and ice creams as he could, and we stopped along the way so that I could have as much sugar-cane juice as I wanted.

12

No matter how many times she let her down or how many lectures she gave her, my mother maintained a relationship with her sister until the day she died. My aunt even sold her place in Dokki so that she could move back to Heliopolis to be closer to my mother and uncle because she loved them both in her way. I was "the most like her" in all the family stories, largely because we'd both done well at school. Her parents didn't dote on her the way they doted on my mother, so she put all her energy into getting a good education and becoming an English teacher, and then when she decided to stop working, she devoted herself to educating her sons. Our two families were carbon-copies: two older sons and a little girl. A trinity in duplicate.

They used to call each other "sister," which was quite uncommon—a noun and no name—and quite traditional; the stress on the familial bond. It occurs to me now that the habit kept them close, like an ancient law that had to be followed regardless of any other feelings under the surface.

The week that I'd spent at her house as a child wasn't what caused me to dislike my aunt permanently. When I was in middle school, we had another significant and decisive confrontation at her house in Heliopolis. I can't remember what caused it. My mother was there, and when my aunt made a comment about something I'd done, she snapped. "Leave my daughter alone. Do you understand?" Mama and I left, slamming the door behind us and ignoring my aunt's angry calls. I later learned that she'd criticized my mother endlessly for my poor upbringing.

One time after she'd heard I was getting married, she was very cruel to my mother, but I was spared since I never said more than hello to her on the occasions when I didn't stay in my room the whole time she was over. My mother looked shaken after she left.

When she was in university, my cousin spent summer vacation at our house to escape her mother's rules. She could open up to my mother, and it was in our house that she was allowed to meet her handsome boyfriend from university. He asked my mother for permission to propose before he'd even met my aunt at the formal occasion. He turned up at our house with several types of cake as though it were the first time he'd ever come over. I was so happy for the young couple when my aunt eventually consented to "the underachiever." They used to kiss with such focus that they'd forget I was even there.

13

"Old-man Ahmad." I see him on TV a lot these days, and it always makes me smile. His hair is grey now, but he's still playing the same role he's always played and he seems content. He likes it when people come up to him in public even if they can't remember exactly which show it was they saw him in. He either plays a good guy or a bad guy—there's not much more to it than that—and I don't even think that many people know his name. I don't talk about him. I like seeing him on TV because it reassures me. I like seeing him in those conventional roles. Maybe he's still looking for his big break. He could be a star overnight. Who knows?

He was friends with my second husband, and after the divorce, he came over and told me that he was very sad about everything that had happened. "The world isn't a bad place," he said. "There are good people out there." He told me I was like a sister to him and that I should think of him as a brother, but our sibling relationship wavered for years because I was repelled by anything that reminded me of the eighteen-month-long marriage. The most hellish thing I'd ever been through. He left me his number and said to get in touch if I needed anything, as though atoning for the crime he'd played no part in. I knew that he hadn't. He didn't need to prove it. He knew my ex-husband from work, and he was never part of his despicable circles, never hung out at the places we used to go. I might have seen him at the theater once. Perhaps he felt a responsibility toward me because he'd once had a small part in a play my ex-husband wrote.

I called him in the evening, and he appeared at our door early the next morning in his Fiat 128. My mother thanked him outlandishly as she rushed to claim the passenger seat. "Thank you so much, Mr. Ahmad. I'm sorry you had to come so early." He assured her that it was no inconvenience at all and that he never went back to sleep after dawn prayers. On the way back after chemotherapy, she was half out of it so she didn't even notice he was there. Though he'd been the one who signed her out of the hospital and set her down carefully in the wheelchair while I packed her bag, and had helped me lift her into the car.

Sometimes she picked fights with me like a cantankerous child when she didn't want to sit in the wheelchair. "I swear to God, if you don't sit down, I'm going to slap you. I swear I'll slap you," I said to her once when I could no longer control myself, but she gave me a look that I'll never forget. In that suppressed rage, my mother came back, and she brought with her our old family dynamic.

Even though she had to lean on the wheelchair, she still managed to push me aside so that she could stagger into her seat. Without anyone's help. That was the only time I spoke to her like that.

It could have been "Old-man Ahmad's" greatest performance, and he wouldn't know it. He was the leading man. Ramzi kept his old yellow Datsun parked outside his in-laws' house, and we'd agreed years before my mother got sick that he'd lend it to us when he was out of town. I learned to drive on that car, and one time when I was driving it, it broke down because of an electrical fault. I called Buthayna's brother to come help me out because he used to cruise with the car before Ramzi lent it to us. I guess he told Ramzi that I'd "ruined" the car or something, so he took it to get fixed, and then it became his after that. No longer mine. That was how Ramzi wanted it. His brother-in-law started driving the car to university and would use it to pick up girls. He used to tell me about the dates he had in that car.

I wish I could have driven my mother back and forth to the hospital in that Datsun. I didn't want to have to ask someone for a ride each time we went. We could have woken up early together to have breakfast, and then I'd place her bag in the trunk. When we got there, I'd park the car, and when the session was over, we'd drive back home together. I cursed Ramzi countless times as I stood outside the Arab Contractors' Hospital waiting for a taxi to deliver new patients so that we could get a ride back home. I hated having to prolong that horrible time when she'd just received a dose of chemotherapy and was sitting in a wheelchair, her head lolling to the side. In an hour or two, she'd wake up in pain. All I wanted was to drive her home, but I knew that wasn't going to happen. I also knew that revenge was a one-way street: one night long ago, as I sat on a marble bench outside the hospital beside my mother while we waited for a taxi, I remembered that my first husband had given me a yellow VW beetle that he didn't use. I went home and told Ramzi, and then we immediately proceeded to devise a schedule for the car. I took it to work in the mornings, and then when I got back, he would drive it to his clinic. A few days later, my husband told me that he wanted to sell the car so that he could buy me a new one, which he never did. I guess Ramzi had seen that coming, so after delivering an angry lecture about how I'd failed to stand up for my marital rights, he stopped speaking to me for a few days.

My writer friend would often send her driver with her fancy Toyota to pick us up at our house and take us to the hospital, where he'd open the door for my mother and then go looking for a wheelchair. He'd pick her up and set her down in the chair with care, and then kneel by her feet and lift each one onto the footrest. On those days, I felt the strongest I've ever felt. The nurses couldn't quite pinpoint my authority, but they couldn't ignore it either as they feared potential consequences. My friend gave me that.

Ramzi came over to congratulate me a month after I received my master's degree. Our mother had died, and that meant that he no longer had the excuse that she got between us. He picked out a photo of me in my robes at the thesis defense and said that he'd keep it on his desk so that his colleagues would see his sister, "the doctor." "You still don't have a car?" he asked me out of nowhere.

I overlooked his total ignorance about my life circumstances and just replied, "How would I, dear?" with a smile.

"So how do you get to university?"

I impersonated a driver. "Microooobussss!"

He was silent for a while, and then he nodded a few times. "Do you want the Datsun? It's pretty old, but it'll get you there."

"I'd love that!"

As he was leaving, he said, "The car's in Buthayna's name, but I'm the one who paid for it," and I didn't let that dampen my joy one bit. My problems were solved! Ramzi said he'd come over the following day so that we could sort everything out, so I woke up at seven in the morning, excited for the car, and excited to see my brother, but he never showed up. Nothing. I found out two days later that he was already back in Saudi Arabia.

14

For years I've had a recurring dream, but the only thing disturbing about it is that I have it over and over. I dream that I have a car. Not like the kind of car I have now, just any car. Then the car disappears, and I spend the whole dream searching for it. It looks different each time, but it's always a car! I once asked a psychologist friend if the car was a metaphor for my life, and she said she was taken aback by my "oversimplification." She proceeded to invite me to spend a day with her exploring the symbolism of the car in my dreams. I promised her that I would take her up on her offer, but I never did. If it had been a nightmare, I might have.

15

Freedom from my memories. It hasn't been easy to write all of this, but the pain only lasts a day. The last effort. Each memory vanishes when I write it down.

It's comforting to know that. From prior experience, I assumed that having written about it, I'd never dream about the yellow Datsun again, the shapeshifting car of my dreams. There was a slight chance that by writing about it, I'd triggered the memory and would start seeing it—not a placeholder car—in my dreams after I turned off the computer and went to bed. The car never appeared, though, so I knew I'd guessed right. It was gone forever.

I woke up this morning feeling like I couldn't breathe. I pushed the cats off me roughly and then did whatever I could to improve my mood. None of it worked. At 8 a.m., all became clear. I shivered, and then a sudden terror came over me. It enveloped me as I walked through the house. I wasn't used to panic attacks. Bouts of depression, I understood—my mind and senses sink until it passes—but panic was different. The last thing I'd written about was the car episode, so I figured it had something to do with that and decided that I would go back to sleep. I shut all the doors so that I didn't hear a peep from the outside world, got into bed, and tried to sleep. Every single sound made my skin crawl. The whole world was on the other side of my bedroom door, about to crash through, and all I wanted to do was disappear—in sleep—for a bit until the storm passed.

I woke up a little while later, and although the panic was gone, my whole body felt exhausted as if I'd been running. As if something had been chasing me. I'm worried about what will happen the next time the car dream visits me. The kiss of terror might have brought it back to life and turned it into a nightmare.

16

My mother loved hearing me say, "I need to sit down and think." She understood that usually meant that I was contemplating a major life decision. After my nasty second marriage ended, she did everything she could to get in touch with Ramzi's old classmates. Out of the ones he'd last been in contact with, whose numbers my mother found in an old address book that Ramzi had left behind, a friend in Germany was the only one we knew. Ramzi had cut ties with all of them after he moved abroad, focusing all his attention on his young family, unable to forget something his wife had said—"Your friends all flirt with me." She may have been telling the truth. Buthayna was a beautiful woman, and men were always turning their heads to look at her when she passed. Ramzi's other friends—the ones he'd shared novels, films, and Sheikh Imam songs with as a young man, the principled ones whom he could trust never to "flirt" with his wife—had vanished, and he never went looking for them. Especially not after he came back from Saudi Arabia with a long musk-scented beard. Under the beard, a new belly protruded from beneath a white tunic. My mother and I exchanged a smirk while Ramzi was telling us about some religious broadcaster, and that irritated him. My mother herself never missed Sheikh al-Shaarawi's program on Fridays because she liked how he explained religious concepts in plain language. From time to time, she'd wrap her hair up in a turban, but I'd tease her about it so that she wouldn't take it too far: "I miss the old you!"

"You'll feel different when you get older," she'd say laughing. She was religious her entire life and never once doubted that there was a god. Whenever I voiced my doubts, she'd announce that "the conversation was over" and storm off.

During Ramadan, we fasted together, and then we'd break our fast at the dining table that Ramzi had bought. Since it was just the two of us, we'd given up on the tray, only using it when the other wasn't at home. We'd sit on the balcony talking until dawn, drinking tea and coffee and offering each other cigarettes. We always had something to talk about, too much to talk about. There was always one more thing that she or I wanted to tell the other, but we'd have to postpone it till the next day. Sometimes they announced the dawn prayer while she was in the middle of smoking a cigarette, but she wouldn't put it out, so I'd let her know that the fast had started. "Do you think they had clocks back in the day? There's only a drag left."

When she finally found his number, Mama called Ramzi's friend without telling me. They were old friends, but Ramzi, the jealous husband, had cut off ties; it now occurs to me that the real reason Ramzi was jealous was because his friend had finished his master's degree and was beginning a doctorate. He had specialized in psychiatry and worked tirelessly at a government hospital, where he'd been recognized with a promotion. He liked me when we were younger, before my first marriage, and while my mother had thought him "a suitable match," Ramzi turned me against him.

"He used to be passionately in love with another girl. Do you really wanna be her stand-in?"

Ramzi had sowed doubt, so I turned him down even after he opened up to me about the other girl and promised me that he was over her. There was nothing more to say. He married a nice girl who stayed at home and gave him boys and girls.

I really respected him, so I immediately agreed when my mother proposed that we go to see him. Curiosity to meet the woman who'd taken my place in his heart may have played a part, as well. He and his wife welcomed us into their home warmly, and his children came out to introduce themselves. Then when he asked to speak to me privately in his office, his wife graciously offered to give my mother a tour of the apartment.

We made several visits to their apartment as he and my mother wove a conspiracy behind my back. He gave her all the signed notes she needed in order to get me enrolled in the university again. I'd given up on it completely because the prospect of going back to the faculty of business was the worst thing I could imagine. I had finally made friends with poets and playwrights, and people were beginning to talk about my work. Published under a new name—mine minus my father's—which I thought sounded catchy.

After the conspiracy was wrapped up successfully, the psychiatrist told me I needed to start over by going back to university. "I'm not Nagla Fathy, and this isn't *The Mirror*," I said sarcastically, but he overlooked the comment. He insisted that I visit him at home, not at his clinic, because he seemed to think that I needed to be surrounded by "family" somehow. He validated our criticisms of Ramzi; he was the one who gave me the key to understanding him: "Ramzi doesn't know how to have deep relationships, not even with his friends. I should know." I relaxed a little after that and then a bit more when he picked up the oud beside him and showed me how much he'd learned to play just from "working it out." He hummed at first and then sang an Umm Kulthum song to me softly. I knew he was a big fan, but I never was.

"Why do you like the line 'I'm jealous of the southerly breeze'? It sucks," I once asked him when we were younger, but this time I listened compliantly.

"I don't understand how a poet can hate that song," he said to me as he placed the oud aside. I'd gone from patient to poet.

"Because it's really bad poetry!"

He nodded. "Fine, forget about that. How can you write poetry if you haven't studied Arabic at university and improved your language skills?"

I sat down and thought about it for a few days before speaking to my mother. I didn't tell her about all the thoughts that had crossed my mind, the many hours I'd spent weighing my options: ending my life, for once and for all—I'd thought about it in such excruciating detail that no one would be able to change my mind. I kept repeating the lines by Cavafy in my head: "Now that you've ruined yourself here, in this corner of the world, you've ruined it wherever else you go". The only other option was to start over. I worried about Mama too much to choose the first. She was older now, and I could picture her after I died: a defeated woman, estranged from one of her sons and a daughter lost to suicide. How could I do that to her?

I don't know if she had any idea of what was going on in my head, but she gave me space to make my decision. She'd bring me meals, sandwiches in the evenings, teas, and coffees and then walk out again in silence. When my aunt came over, they'd sit in her bedroom with the door shut because Mama didn't want me to overhear anything my aunt said. "You're coddling her as usual. That's why she's like this in the first place!" When I finally emerged from my bedroom, I announced my decision gruffly: "I'll go back and finish my degree, but not in business. That's my only condition."

"Business? Haha, no that ship has sailed," she replied as she was beating eggs. "Dr. Ali and I already took your application to the Arabic department. Just let me finish this cake and make a prayer of gratitude, and then I'll call him. He'll be happy."

17

The ping-pong ball on my mother's chest grew to the size of an orange, firm and unmissable. It no longer caused pain, so she'd stopped using the rheumatism ointment, and now only bothered her in the summers, when she'd cut a hole in her galabiyya so that she could keep it uncovered. It was a shocking sight, but we kept our reactions to ourselves once we got used to it. No one could continue to claim that it was rheumatism or a rare fungus. Even Ramzi had to bite his tongue. Whenever Mama or I expressed our skepticism about the diagnosis, he just changed the subject. After ten years of wandering—of doing everything and nothing—I had finally got my life back on track. Ramzi, Buthayna, and their four daughters spent the summer holidays with us when they came back from Saudi Arabia because he was "still saving up." He longed for a son, and Buthayna kept his hopes up. They slept in the back bedroom together with the infant between them while their other three daughters slept in the cramped sitting room next to the bathroom. Mama and I had to be careful not to kick them on our way to the bathroom in the middle of the night.

Ramzi was always complaining that he was short of money, but at one point he started talking about a new investment idea. A friend of his had told me that he'd had to remind Ramzi that some of his certificates of deposit were coming due because he was too busy working to remember things like that. It had sounded credible to me, but when I told my mother, she refused to believe it. She didn't think Ramzi would conceal his fortune from her. At least not after we'd told him, as we had a few years earlier, that he had to start sending us a fixed sum of money each month instead of the tiny amounts he used to send whenever he felt like it. At the time, he'd protested that his work wasn't predictable and his finances weren't in great shape.

Ramzi's new scheme was to buy some desert land near the road connecting Cairo and Alexandria and develop it for agriculture. It took several days before he could find someone to dig a well, and he and Buthayna's brother and father had to drive out there every other day during his vacation to get things moving. A few days before he headed back to Saudi Arabia, he asked to speak to me one on one. Something that hadn't happened in years. He came across as very kind when he explained to me that he'd put all the land in Buthayna's name, but that he'd insisted to her that she should give me five of the plots if anything were to happen to him. There was no way he'd dream of going against Islamic practice when it came to that sort of thing. I had never imagined being part of a conversation like that, but despite my shock, I tried to put him at ease.

"I hope you have a very long life, Brother, but if anything ever happens to you, I'll get a job and make sure your girls are looked after."

He repeated himself all the same: "I gave her very clear instructions. This is God's way."

They returned to Saudi Arabia shortly after that, leaving the agricultural enterprise to Buthayna's father and brother. Her brother was still in university, so everyone thought it made sense for him to have the yellow Datsun to take him back and forth to his provincial university and the farm.

The land remained barren. The only thing they managed to grow was weeds, and after several years,

Buthayna's father and brother sold it off using the power of attorney Ramzi had given them and took a cut for themselves in exchange for their hard work. His own share was a pittance.

Mama and I would have never dared say, "Your in-laws ripped you off," not even to get back at Buthayna, who'd told him, "Your brother ripped you off" all those years ago. That had made my mother cry for days. She and I both knew that Ramzi would defend his wife's family no matter what.

18

Mama got very excited when Ramzi offered to bring her to Saudi Arabia so that she could perform the pilgrimage after years of making vague promises. I told her that I wasn't sure she should be traveling so soon after her second operation, but she just ignored me. It was like she was going on a school trip. She couldn't stop talking about it. She promised over and over that she'd take good care of herself, and I had no choice but to yield to her exuberance. Throughout her long absence, the house felt empty, but I refused to go out, for no reason other than that I didn't want to. I preferred to wait at home for a letter from her in which she'd describe her visit to the Kaaba and tell me that she never stopped praying for me. The trip had reignited the fear of losing her that had gripped me years before, but when I went to pick her up at the airport, the tiny woman on the other side of the glass darting around and grabbing her own bags off the conveyer belt didn't seem like my mother at all! She was dressed in a long white robe, and she'd slimmed down while she'd been away. We embraced for a long time, and I could tell she was thrilled to see me. On the drive home, she told me breathlessly all about her trip. I had been looking forward to her return with great anticipation and had cleaned the house, so that it would be sparkling when she got home, prepared a meal, and ordered ice cream. Ice cream was the only thing she ate with real gusto, without any abnegation. One time, I remember asking her if she would share, but she couldn't meet my eye as she confessed that she'd finished it all. "I just couldn't stop myself."

When we arrived at the house, she unpacked her luggage so that she could show me the fabrics she'd bought for me—"If I could've, I'd have brought you back the whole world"—and then she handed me two whole outfits by famous, fashionable brands—"These are from your brother." I marveled at his sudden generosity, and immediately went to try them on. Finally, we came to sit on the balcony, side by side, drinking tea. She recounted to me some of the arguments she'd had with Ramzi and told me how sweet Buthayna had been, which is what I'd expected. When I wasn't around, Buthayna treated my mother like her own.

It wasn't uncommon for Ramzi to send me an outfit or two from time to time, but his grandest gift came after my second divorce. After he'd already paid for all the new furniture. He bought me several outfits and new shoes and a handbag. At first, I thought he was trying to win me over for some reason I couldn't understand, but Buthayna quickly stamped out the joy I'd been feeling. "The clothes look great on you. We got the exact same stuff for my sister, as well."

19

Some days change your life. They don't have a particular shape or color, and we never see them coming because they're just like any other. And because we always fail to notice when something in our lives has got stuck. On one such day, Mama and I went with my cousin to visit a famous oncologist because my aunt had given her an ultimatum during her last weekly visit. "'A fungus?' That's rubbish. I swear if you don't go see this doctor, I'll never step foot in this house again." I understand why my mother was afraid to go—she knew what was happening. I'm certain of it. She used to tell me about the bone cancer that had killed her mother's sister and nearly killed her mother. The orange on her chest, which grew a little each day, was taunting her.

When she heard the diagnosis, her legs gave out so I had to hold her upright. She howled, and she didn't care who was watching as my cousin and I hovered around her and tried to calm her down. In the days preceding the consultation, we'd been busy getting new tests done and re-doing the old ones like the new doctor had requested. Mama couldn't remember where she'd hidden one of the old tests, but she informed us of the results. The oncologist usually refrained from disparaging the work of his colleagues, but he couldn't believe what he was hearing. "A fungus! What was he even thinking? We could have done something!" She'd regained her composure a bit by the time we arrived back at the house, and within a couple of hours, her determination replenished, she was asking me to call Ramzi and deliver the news.

20

Nothing was worse than when Ramzi came to stay with us over the summer, especially after I'd gone back to university. At the end of the academic year, my mother would wait for me on the balcony like she used to wait for my brothers when they were taking the university entrance exams. The only difference was that the sullen expression she'd worn back then had given way to a sunny one. From the first year onward, she waited impatiently for the only sound she wanted to hear: "Passed with merit!" Having already prepared refreshments, she'd pass them out to the neighbors, who took part in the celebration. "With merit! The second highest grades on the exam! She'll be at the top of the class next year!" But the joyful atmosphere would soon be forgotten.

In the summer, the house would fill with kids, running and screaming. Ramzi would take the new color television into his bedroom, and Mama would struggle with the antenna on her old black-and-white one. I usually went out to escape everyone. Mama always let me go out; she just needed to know when I'd be back so that she wouldn't worry about me. She let me go on trips with my girlfriends and would let me stay at Ra'ifa's house for a week or more to prepare for the upcoming academic year, which was two months away. Ramzi no longer took any interest in my life. He never asked where I was going or where I'd spent the night. When I was younger, I knew that he wanted me to grow up "free" and that "he trusted me," so it made sense that I'd opened up to him about my crushes and asked for his advice, but things changed after my second divorce. After I'd heard him say, "I swear if he tries to do anything to my wife and kids." I could tell that he'd washed his hands of me, and I knew how to distinguish between trust and indifference.

In the final two years of my degree, Ramzi and his wife allowed me to use their bedroom while they were away because it was located at the back of the house away from the street, so it was a better environment for both study and sleep. In the summers, I moved back into the bedroom at the front, where I could never sleep because of the commotion that the children made in the street outside—that is, on the other side of the wall.

21

"They'll be gone in less than two months," Mama and I would say to each other when we felt exhausted. By that point, I'd been back at university for three years and was about to take my final exams, which would determine whether I was offered a teaching job after graduation, and my chances seemed very good. That was when the oncologist informed us of the devastating diagnosis.

Mama went into overdrive every year when exam season approached. She'd buy meat and chicken with money she'd saved from her pension all year so that I would be "well nourished" during my exams. She'd tell her friends not to visit because I was studying and would go to see them at their houses instead. I woke up at dawn on exam days, having gone to bed at ten, so that I could pray and study a bit more before I had to leave. On my way out, I'd lean down so that she could place her hand on top of my head and say a prayer for me.

Mama stayed up all night so that she could wake me up at dawn. She waited with the lights off, the volume of the television turned down to a whisper. A vigil. I begged her to just set an alarm and go to sleep, but she wouldn't have it. "No, I'm going to stay up. We can't afford to oversleep!"

22

A few days later, when it was confirmed that the cancer was in her thyroid, my mother's nerves settled a bit. That hell seemed more obliging than the other. "I'm just glad that it isn't in the bone." Possible treatments were floated optimistically and everyone got to share their opinion—not just the doctors, but our family, friends, and neighbors, as well. Mama's decision, when it came, was final, though: there would be no chemotherapy and no radiation, just radioactive iodine therapy followed by three days in the hospital, and that was that.

She'd made her mind up about another thing, too, which she considered even more important, and she wouldn't let Ramzi, my aunt, or me try to persuade her otherwise. "I'm not going to start my treatment until your exams are done. I've had this issue for years, so a month isn't going to make any difference." I felt guilty, of course. "Do you really want to throw away all our hard work? Just finish your exams, and I promise I'll go to the hospital the very next day."

She got her way, but when Ramzi and his family arrived the following month, he made a snide remark to me about her having to put her treatment off until my exams were done. Mama was furious, so she told

Ramzi she wanted to speak to him in private and then she let him have it like she'd never done before. That was at least how she described it as she tried to console me. Ramzi himself came into my bedroom later that evening to give me a hug and apologize. "We're trying to beat cancer here, so our guilt complexes have to wait till later. Don't be upset. I'm sorry for what I said."

23

The iodine therapy wasn't painful, and my mother's doctor—whom the other doctors, even the older ones, all called "Professor"—was somewhat nice. We'd first met him at the Arab Contractors' Hospital when we were sent there for a final round of tests. He found time to speak to me and listen to my concerns, and he reassured me that Mama's case wasn't severe and that there was a chance she could be cured, especially because she was still in her sixties. I packed her bag and then the next day, we went to the hospital, where all they asked her to do was drink a solution. I stepped out of the room quickly like the doctor had instructed in order to protect myself from the radiation, but Mama had to stay there for three days all by herself. I slept with the telephone beside my bed in case—God forbid—anyone from the hospital called in the middle of the night.

We got Mama a private room for the first two sessions like she'd insisted because we were already getting a big discount due to Ramzi being in the doctors' union. He paid for the costs of the first two sessions, but as the date of the third session drew near, I had to send him several messages through his father-in-law to remind him that any delay in treatment could allow the cancer to spread. At the very last minute, there was a knock at the door one evening, and I knew I could breathe again. It was Ramzi's father-in-law carrying an envelope, which contained the exact amount of the hospital bill. Not a penny more.

There was no private room for her third session. Mama had to share with another patient who "wouldn't shut up" and "snored all night," so she'd been unable to sleep. Nonetheless, I was able to convince her that a private room would be extravagant, and when I went to pick her up, I found her and her roommate acting like best buddies, making plans to see each other outside of the hospital.

The post-treatment phase was always the hardest, but the various tasks got divided up among those closest to us more quickly than I'd anticipated. My friend Ra'ifa was in charge of labs: she'd drive the nurse over to our house so she could take blood from my mother, and then she'd return a few days later with the results. She always refused to tell me how much she'd paid, so I accepted her kindness with gratitude. My aunt informed her children—in particular her two sons who'd earned doctorates in engineering—that they would be covering the costs of the MRI scans and small incidentals like taxi fare if we failed to find someone who could lend us a car.

Mama's anxiety was the worst part, though. She was terrified of the sounds that came out of the MRI machine that wrapped around her head. "It's like being tormented in your grave." And there was my anxiety, too. I had to lock it up in my bedroom after I heard the doctor explain that although the cancer had spread, he was hopeful that they'd be able to wipe out the secondary tumors in the next session.

The worst was the fear that gripped me as I pushed my way into the radiology room—ignoring the nurses' warnings—so that I could help my mother into the wheelchair because I'd watched one of the nurses drop her into it like a sack of potatoes the last time we were there.

Before her treatment had even begun, I'd promised her, swearing on the Quran, that I wouldn't conceal anything about her condition from her, and I didn't. "I'm not an idiot and I'm not a child, so don't you dare hide anything from me." I did choose my words very carefully, however, as I communicated the truth and I always pre-assured her before sharing any new developments. I lied to her exactly once. Just before the fifth session, the doctor informed me that the cancer had spread into her bones, and the room began to spin. How could I tell her that the curse had materialized? What would I do with her agony? My mother was resilient, but news like that could have been the final straw. It didn't matter that the doctor was so confident. "It's a secondary tumor. We'll get it. You'll see."

That night, after making certain that she was asleep, I went into my bedroom, shut the door behind me, and banged my head against the wall over and over quickly. I didn't stop until I felt numb.

24

Peering at the test results from behind his grand desk, the oncologist suddenly looked up at me and grinned.

"It's no longer in the bone. We got it! Am I allowed to say 'I told you so'?" He softened when I began crying uncontrollably, and walked over and patted me on the head. "Didn't you tell me you were writing your MA thesis about poetry? You poets have soft hearts. You've got to toughen up a little. You'll never get your PhD, if you don't." He was like a real father, and all I wanted was to bow down and kiss his hand, but he just walked to the door and flashed a smile. "Alright then. Off you go. Have fun and study hard. I've got other patients."

Mama was asleep in her room, so I took a nap, as well, and then later she asked me to rub Voltaren cream onto her back to soothe the pain. I managed to keep my cool for a month, but it wasn't easy. Every time she mentioned a pain in her bones, I tried to change the subject. "Give me a break, sister. Cancer and arthritis at the same time?" I played my part so well that she never once suspected that I was keeping a secret from her, not even as the pain in her bones intensified.

When the oncologist learned that my brother was also a physician, he asked to meet him, so Ramzi came back to visit for a couple of days, and he was the one who got the unvarnished truth: It was true that the tumor, whose progress my mother and I monitored fervently, had shrunk, but the current treatment wasn't going to cure her completely. If the cancer cells began growing again over the next twelve months, she'd have to have surgery. Ramzi told the doctor that he would convey the prognosis to the patient himself. At home, I informed Ramzi that I'd been hiding one aspect of our mother's condition from her because I was afraid that she'd spiral.

When he came back after speaking to her in private for a bit, he looked distressed. "I told her about the bone cancer," he confessed like a guilty child. I was struck dumb for a few seconds, but then I exploded. I don't remember exactly what I said except that he'd ruined everything on purpose and that I'd never ever forgive him. He replied that as a physician, he didn't see any point in concealing the details of a patient's condition from them before slamming the door behind him on his way out.

When I went into my mother's bedroom, I found her lying in bed serenely as if she hadn't heard a sound, least of all our raised voices ringing through the house. When I leaned over to fuss with the pillows she was lying on, she pushed my hand away gently and re-arranged them herself. "Is he gone?" I nodded. Then as I turned to leave, I heard her say, "I'm never going to believe anything you say again. You swore on the Quran." Her words like a sharp blade.

The storm passed after a few days, and she softened. Ramzi had come to see her the following day on his way to the airport while I was sleeping, and they agreed to wait until the sessions were over before they made any decisions about surgery. Everything was deferred. In the evening, Mama and I watched television side by side on the daybed, where I'd squeezed myself in beside her, and later when I refused to go sleep in my own bed, she held me in her arms and we fell together into slumber.

25

There were three songs that we tried to keep out of the house: "Bird of Passage" by Nagat, "I Wish You'd Come

Back" by Abdel Halim Hafez, and my mother's favorite, "Do They Still Remember?" by Farid El-Atrash. Whenever any of them played on the radio or on TV, I'd scurry over to shut the device off because they always left her in a deep depression. Those songs, like the smell of grilled meat on Eid, reminded her of the son she'd lost. She had no idea where he was, but she refused to believe that he was dead.

She'd taken to sitting in her bedroom alone when she wanted to write, but it was something that she'd done her entire life. She'd filled entire notebooks, including the covers, with her thoughts and lines of free verse, but when she got ill, she decided that she wanted to write a novel based on her own life, in order perhaps to liberate herself from it —just as I'm doing now. She even read some short passages out to me.

On New Year's Eve one year during her illness, she allowed me to grill meat for the girlfriends I planned to have over. The ritual had been taboo ever since Ragi left, but it seemed to have lost its sanctity over the years. Her stance on alcohol never softened, though, and whenever it came up, she'd remind me of how her father had treated her mother and how my father had bankrupted us to feed his addiction. When I told my friends that they wouldn't be allowed to drink even a beer at our house on New Year's, all but one or two declined my invitation, and even the ones who did come made a point of telling me that the only reason they'd turned down their other invitations—to parties with toasts!—was because they didn't want me to spend New Year's Eve on my own.

Personally, I didn't find it an inconvenience. Ever since my mother had been diagnosed, I'd been feeling that her survival depended on how well I behaved somehow. During my second marriage, Mama used to get very distraught when she'd go into our bedroom to tidy up and find empty bottles and glasses strewn about, but she never said anything to me about it. When we got the diagnosis, I prayed to God and promised Him through tears that I wouldn't touch a drop of alcohol if He spared her from pain. I begged Him to punish me if I broke my promise, and after pressing my forehead against the carpet and taking a deep breath, I sensed that my offer had been accepted.

For seven years, I socialized sober. The friends who knew me when I used to drink would tease me, and they once even went so far as to put a few drops of wine in my drink. I leapt to my feet and ran to wash my mouth out as if I'd been poisoned.

After my mother died and the three nights of mourning had passed, my writer friend took me to Alexandria to see the sea. I sat on a wooden chair, staring out at the horizon, my memory wiped clean, burying my bare toes in the sand. I told my friend about the promise I'd made—"And now it's over." She understood what I needed, so the waiter appeared with a cold bottle of beer that he placed on the small table beside me. The first sip sliced through me like a knife.

26

After reviewing my file, the department decided not to offer me a position, so I worked even harder in my third year to get to the top of the class and I succeeded. It was in my final year that we learned of my mother's diagnosis—or rather faced up to the truth. I felt guilty that my mother had postponed her treatment for a month for the sake of my exams, but getting a job as a teaching assistant would have changed my life. When I'd gone back to university, the most I'd hoped for was a bachelor's degree so that I could get an office job and put an end to the snide remarks, but the more I studied, the bigger my dreams grew, and it felt like they were beginning to pass me by, so I chased after them.

It would have been poetic justice. A new job so that I'd feel more secure as I embarked on the more difficult challenge of my mother's treatment, but the department chair, a solemn and domineering figure, had vowed that I would never get a position in the department as long as he was a member. There was no personal animosity between us because I was a corresponding student and I only went into the department when I had to take exams. They may not have seen me in lectures, but they encountered me elsewhere: at poetry festivals and on the posters for a play I'd written. I'd taken a class with one of the department chair's former students and when I bumped into him in the hallway after one of my exams, he made a jibe that had shaken me. "You better not get your hopes up. The whole thing is like musical chairs." His comment made me wince a bit because he, of all people, would know.

"What makes you say that, Professor?"

"You don't come to lectures."

"Because I'm a corresponding student."

"It doesn't matter. We're free to notice which students turn up and which ones are too busy loafing at home."

"I haven't been loafing at home! My mother has cancer," I protested, perhaps with too much restraint.

"I'm sorry to hear that," he said. "But everyone's got someone sick in their family."

I didn't sleep that night. I only had one exam left, which was the exam for his class, but that wasn't what kept me up. My grade didn't matter; the writing was on the wall. But I couldn't get over the humiliation. I'd felt feeble, and my voice had quavered. I'd struggled to spit out the word cancer, which I said to him in English as though it was something embarrassing. Like a beggar showing off his amputated legs to people walking past. My mother managed to soothe my nerves, and by the end of our conversation, her prayers for his ill fortune had me in stitches. I managed to leap the last hurdle—not with distinction, of course, but with merit—and because of the other distinctions I'd received, it didn't really affect my overall grade.

In their game of "musical chairs," the girl who had been fifth in the class landed the top spot on account of her "outstanding final-year performance." She ended up with two points more than me overall. The three other girls in the top five against whom I'd competed for the past four years were as shocked as I was. They'd worked so hard to beat me in our final year exams only to learn that the real decisions were made behind closed doors.

The only professor in the department who was unhappy with the outcome was a wonderful man who steered clear of power struggles and devoted all his attention to research. He told me he was sad that he hadn't been able to stop them and encouraged me to keep going. Over time, he and my mother would become friends. Whenever I spoke to him on the phone, he'd ask to speak to her, and if he'd called when I was out, he and my mother would often chat about this and that, as she'd happily report to me when I got back home.

He was the one who told me about the department chair's vow and about the other professors' concerns—or better yet, insistence—that I would corrupt the female students. "The last thing we need is a bohemian poet."

I had no idea that the whole thing had already been decided two years earlier when I took part in a poetry festival in another Arab country. Out on the lobby balcony at the hotel they put us up at, I had run into a senior professor at another university. "Good morning, Professor. What brings you here?"

"Oh, I'm just getting some sun. I hardly got any sleep last night." He then proceeded to tell me, with a smile on his face, how he'd spent the whole night persuading his colleagues—the chair of my department and his little sidekick—not to leave. They had already re-packed their bags in protest when they discovered that a second-year student of theirs had been invited to the same festival as they had. It took a while, but he managed to convince them that the organizers had invited me in my capacity as a poet and that no one else cared that I was a student in their department.

The rest of the festival went smoothly because they just ignored me, and I avoided them, but I guess I was naïve. They held their resentment in check for the next two years and then it blew up in my unsuspecting face.

I left the department and enrolled for a master's at another fine institution, where the important professors all welcomed me as one would a poet who was beginning to gain some traction.

27

When I began working at a literary quarterly, I found myself with new friends and colleagues, and I got a decent honorarium every three months, which I was happy to hand over to Mama although she resisted at first. She claimed that we could get by on her and my father's pensions and that I should keep the money for myself, but I had very strong feelings on the subject. She seemed a bit embarrassed taking the money, so to make her feel better about it, I told her I wanted an increase in "my allowance." That made everything okay. Shortly before I got paid, we'd sit together and plan out how we were going to spend the money, drawing up lists of the things we needed but couldn't afford. Ramzi sent money for the radioactive iodine therapy, and the rest of the expenses were covered by my friend Ra'ifa and my aunt's two sons. My mother and I had a good time on the few days when I arrived home with my honorarium and her favorite, a big carton of ice cream. "Mama, you and I make a happy couple." She gave me a kiss in agreement. "If only they would leave us alone."

28

When the radioactive iodine therapy was over, tests showed that the tumor was under control. It hadn't been knocked out completely, but my mother's advanced age—she was in her seventies by then—meant it was growing slowly, according to the doctors. We spent a few quiet months together as a happy couple. Mama took great interest in the poems I was writing and she always loved to give me feedback on the new ones. I could tell when she didn't like something I'd written because she was usually so enthusiastic, and instead she'd say things like, "Sometimes I just can't get what you're saying, dear. I'm old and I don't always understand the words you use." I could tell when she was lying, so I knew when to discard a bad one. The enthusiasm would return as soon as I brought her something new, though. It didn't matter if she was deep into a nap: if she heard me scratching at the door because I wasn't sure if she was awake, she'd bolt up, rubbing her eyes. "A new poem! Come in! Come in! I'm awake. Do you hear me, dear? Do you hear me?"

Ramzi didn't wait for summer that year. He and his family moved in with us when he quit his job at the hospital after an argument. Mama offered to share the pension income that she and I received with Ramzi, so for the first time ever, our household shared the same meals. Ramzi cooked because Buthayna didn't like to and had already intimated to him that there was a difference between cooking for her family and waiting on her husband's mother and sister. He planned out the entire week's meals, which he cooked in large pots like in camp kitchens, dicing the meat finely so that there would be enough to go around. He needed to act like he had things under control because he didn't know how long the crisis would last. He told me he didn't even know if he'd get another job offer in Saudi Arabia. Mama didn't object to the invasion of her kitchen like she had when my second husband moved in, even though she loved to cook. There's never been anyone better. I can still remember the prayers that the neighbors heaped on me as a child whenever she'd task me with carrying a tray of food over. She just withdrew in silence. Before Ramzi and his family had arrived, she'd been keeping herself busy by cooking meals and teaching me difficult recipes that I hadn't learned when I was younger. Mama believed that people could learn to cook at any age and that little girls belonged at school, not in the kitchen.

I was the one who spoke up. I once told her that the cheap oil Ramzi used made me want to throw up, and the next thing I knew a tray of food appeared in my bedroom, filling the air with the mouthwatering aroma of clarified butter, tasting of my mother's spirit. She made it clear to Ramzi that I didn't have to eat the same food as everyone else.

29

Between radioactive iodine sessions, my mother would return to the autobiographical novel that she was writing. Every month or two, she'd read out new passages to me and I'd tell her what I thought of them. She loved getting positive feedback, but whenever I had something negative to say, she'd take the notebook back and say, "I don't care if it's bad. I'm writing it for myself."

I never interrupted her when she was writing. If there was wet laundry in the bathtub and not on the line, that meant she'd started a new scene. She wasn't a temperamental writer like me. She'd learned to conceal her anger, and more importantly—as she'd later explain to me—she'd learned to conceal her fear, no matter what she was going through. I would've thought she was just trying to boost my spirits if I hadn't seen her in action. She faced one thing after the other, but each time she just accepted it, like her mother before her, whispering, "God help me," to herself. She was even able to transcend her physical being. One time, during her final session, the nurse, who'd come to insert a cannula, was having trouble finding a vein. "I'm sorry I had to poke you so many times, darling. Please just be patient with me."

"Of course. Of course, my dear. When do I say anything other than 'of course'?" She replied in a voice that wasn't hers. I know that I failed to stand up for her. I didn't make a scene or insist that the nurse call the doctor like I'd seen other women do. Mama and I did our best not to complain or spoil our good relations with the nurses. On some level, we realized that we weren't guests. This was our new home—a rental—and they were the landlords, so we had better keep our voices down.

We kept our voices down at home, too, nearly all the time. During Ramzi and his family's long stay, my mother lost her temper exactly once. Behaving like I was indeed her aunt, I'd told my niece off about something she was doing, so she went to complain to her parents about it. Ramzi came out to confront me, and because he raised his voice, I raised mine, and then the next thing I knew, he was insulting me in front of Buthayna and the girls. I stormed out and went straight to Ra'ifa's house as usual. When I called Mama to let her know I was okay, she begged me to come back and swore to me that she'd given Ramzi a serious talking-to. It must have worked because he hugged me very tightly when I got home.

I never fought with Buthayna. We circled each other silently, occasionally displaying affection, but it was very flimsy—the kind of affection that shatters at the first sign of turbulence.

Mama, on the other hand, flew off the handle once, and I'm not talking about the time that she gave Ramzi a lecture about not treating me like a child and speaking to me respectfully in front of his children. I'll never forget it. I was in my bedroom with the door shut, and Mama was in hers with the door ajar. The only sound you could hear was Ramzi talking to his brother-in-law by the front door. "Sure, whatever you want. You're the only brother I've got." As soon as Ramzi shut the door behind him, I heard a roar. "Your brother? He's your brother? The only brother you've got? What about your real brother? Did you forget about him?" Ramzi went into Mama's bedroom to try to calm her down, but I chose not to intervene because I didn't want him to accuse me of taking her side or stirring things up. I wasn't a fan of his in-laws because they were always over at our house, which they treated like their own, but I couldn't help but sympathize with Ramzi. It wasn't his fault that his own brother had disappeared almost twenty years earlier. I'd also forgotten about my brother, and I was worried that our mother would sense it if I said anything in Ramzi's defense. Not that she could drag me into it, though. I was still only a child when he left, whereas Ragi and Ramzi were like twins.

30

I was sitting on a marble bench in the garden outside Heliopolis Hospital one time when Ramzi came out, beaming, and sat down beside me. When I asked about Mama, he said she was getting dressed and was waiting for me to take her home. The smile on his face had lifted my spirits, so I asked him, "How did it go?" as I got to my feet.

"I came out to tell you the good news! She isn't going to need chemotherapy, just radiation. He's such a good doctor. Did I tell you that he—"

Before Ramzi could rattle off all the doctor's achievements, I interrupted him: "So she's cured? What happened to the tumor?"

"Thank God. Thank God," he said, but not in reply to my question. It felt like he was talking to himself. "There's no way I could've paid for the chemotherapy. I'm lucky I just got another job in Saudi Arabia. I wouldn't have been able to afford it."

It felt like I'd been stabbed in the heart. I was stunned for a moment, but then I asked him, "Are you saying that if the doctor had told us she needed chemotherapy, you would have refused?"

"Yes, I would have," he said, looking back at me defiantly. "One of my colleagues has to send his wife money for chemotherapy every month, and it's ruined him. Only God is omnipotent. I just can't, I'm sorry."

When I went in to collect Mama, she was overjoyed at the news she'd received, especially the part when the doctor had told her that the radiation therapy wouldn't hurt. "It just burns a little," she told me. "No big deal. I'll just put some ointment on it. You're going to have to bring me here twice a week," she said. "I hope that's okay."

Ramzi died a month ago or he died that afternoon, one or the other. Did I lay him out on the marble bench in the garden of the hospital with the same hands that I'm using to write this? Then how come his corpse visited my heart so many times in the years after our mother died? Why wasn't I able to write a word of this until I'd heard he was dead?

31

I eventually found steady work, and while it wasn't exactly academic, it did come with the title of "teaching assistant," so my mother handed out celebratory refreshments to the neighbors. Despite having to use a cane and moving with difficulty, she was still very alert, still able to experience joy and pain.

She had stopped asking around if anyone had plans to travel to Germany and had given up waiting for Ragi to walk through the door, but she never entertained the possibility that he could be dead. I was completely convinced.

When I handed her my wages, she only resisted briefly before accepting it, and she gave me a healthy "allowance" in return. We were getting better, and quicker, at making decisions together.

The radiation sessions were a drag, and so were the trips back and forth to the hospital, even though it was quite close to our house. Each time, I had to show gratitude to the various good-hearted cab drivers who helped me escort my mother. My new job was near the pyramids, and I had to be there four days a week, so I'd asked a kind neighbor to check in on my mother from time to time throughout the day. The radiation therapy left scars, which my mother slathered with ointment, and when she drew my attention to some new blue spots on her skin, I reminded her that the doctor had explained that bruising was a possible side-effect and that as long as they didn't hurt, there was nothing to worry about.

We were both terrified of the pain. The horrible pain that she'd seen rack her mother. She hadn't had to face it, so we tried not to think about it, but it kept me up at night. When I couldn't sleep, I'd stay up in my bedroom chain-smoking until I passed out. What if she starts screaming right this second? Once she starts, she'll never stop. The demon in her chest will run wild, filling every corner of the house, ushering the two of us toward hell.

One morning after the blue spots appeared, I got a phone call at work. "I'm bleeding," she said calmly. "Hurry back." I tried to ask for more details, but her voice had gone faint, and I realized that time was of the essence. I grabbed my bag, told my colleagues that I had an emergency at home, and ran out without even informing my boss. As I waited in the street for a taxi, it felt like my mother's life was hanging in the balance. I screamed when I got back home and found blood smudged on the floor and walls of her bedroom, but she just smiled at me awkwardly. She didn't look sick, but like a survivor, and she'd survived more than just the bleed. That was when I realized that she'd been worried that I was going to tell her she was being dramatic. It took seeing my panic for her to allow herself to be terrified as she pointed to the blue spots on her skin from which fountains of blood were spurting, splashing us both.

32

I called my boss to apologize for leaving work without telling him and to ask for some time off—at least a week—, and he said he was very sorry to hear that my mother's health had taken a turn, but I could tell that the request irritated him, so later that same evening, I decided to quit.

I didn't resign in protest against his tetchiness. I simply didn't know what awaited me. All I knew was that for the foreseeable future I'd be in the position of having to ask for time off whenever something happened to my mother. For days, all I could think about was the blood I'd seen, but that wasn't the only reason I quit. The title of my job was teaching assistant, but what I actually did four days a week was go to an office near the pyramids, where teaching assistants and lecturers translated educational materials. My job was to edit the translations, which I received page-by-page, but after I earned a reputation for being painstaking, they started handing me their rough drafts to edit. At first, I was so keen that I even took my work home with me, and it got to the point that my boss, the one who ran the whole publishing house, would ask me to revise the faxes that people sent him for clarity and organization before he read them, and to touch up the remarks he was planning to give at different book festivals.

We had no students. Our enterprise was publishing books, and my responsibility was to make sure that the books we put out looked professional and well written.

On the day that I sent in my resignation, my boss called me at the house and told me that he wasn't going to acknowledge receiving it yet so that I'd have a little more time to think it over.

I certainly didn't need it. I didn't want to prettify anything, didn't want to "make things sound right." I knew I wouldn't be up to it. The ugliness that surrounded me was overwhelming: the hospital smell, my mother's blood, her stinking wounds.

I went back to living off of my father's pension and the money I got from working at the quarterly. The editor was very understanding of everything that I was going through and always allowed me to miss work, even without his permission, if I needed to. My colleagues used to deliver my honorarium to the house even though I'd left them to shoulder the entire issue.

33

The latest development left us with three options: (a) let her bleed to death, (b) make her undergo another surgery, or (c) start chemotherapy.

The first option was unacceptable to me, of course, and it hadn't even occurred to me until the emergency doctor whom I'd summoned from a nearby hospital suggested it. Later when we met with my mother's doctor at the hospital, he sent us to see a famous surgical oncologist, who then sent us to a famous cardiac surgeon, who then sent us to a famous plastic surgeon, before the three of them got together to plan a surgery in which each had an assigned part.

At our meeting with the team of surgeons, the oncologist listened to the plan that they'd hatched and then told us he thought it was foolish. My aunt's son happened to be back in Cairo on vacation at the time, so he took my mother to the best oncologist in the city for another opinion. When she got back, Mama was animated and exuberant. "He's so smart that doctor!" She told me that he'd dropped the pretense of collegiality and spoken very plainly. "What makes him think that there's no point in doing the surgery? He should just admit that he doesn't know how to do it. Let's be serious." When my mother expressed her concerns about her doctor's description of "the extreme pain she'd experience after the surgery," he couldn't conceal his sarcasm, which she enjoyed imitating for my benefit: "Don't listen to him, dear. We do operations like this all the time, so there's nothing to worry about. Tell your doctor I said that he's overdoing it. We have very powerful painkillers at our disposal."

It appeared that the decision had already been taken, so I confessed that I was worried about how Ramzi would react. "Don't worry, I'll take care of it," my cousin responded. "I'll call him and let him know that we can split the cost, even if I have to put in a bit more."

34

Ramzi didn't call me or my mother. He called my friend Ra'ifa, and to this day, she still refuses to tell me exactly what he said. She just repeats what she said at the time: that he used very harsh language to express his anger about the humiliating position we'd put him in. We were forcing him to accept charity and we'd made him look like a child by recruiting his cousin to "get him to face up to his responsibilities."

After she managed to calm him down, Ra'ifa asked Ramzi what he was planning to do. He said he was leaning against it and then slammed the phone down.

After much discussion, Mama and I decided that she wouldn't have the surgery. It would have cost a lot of money, more than my cousin could afford, and even if we'd been able to raise money from friends, it wouldn't have covered Ramzi's "third." Third because one of my friends had offered to split the expenses with Ramzi and my cousin three-ways. "Thirty thousand is doable," he'd said, but neither my mother nor I could "do" it. Her feelings about the surgery had changed completely after she'd spoken to Ramzi. Her former optimism and enthusiasm had given way to total refusal—a stubborn refusal I wasn't able to crack. "What if I really do have extreme pain after the surgery?" I didn't try very hard to persuade her. Impassable walls separated us from the dream of recovery. Pain, impoverishment, the unknown.

35

My old nanny Auntie Saadeya used to visit us from time to time. I still have a black-and-white photo of her as a young woman: smiling, her long hair down to her shoulders, dressed in a blouse and skirt that suited her dark complexion. The photo was probably taken at our house in Alf Maskan shortly before we moved. In the picture, Auntie Saadeya is standing in the kitchen beside the refrigerator, an array of pots and pans hanging above the stovetop behind her. She was the only person whom my mother trusted to look after me because she genuinely treated me like her own daughter. She treated everyone with integrity, even the young men who harassed her in the street. She used to take me to the garden where she'd feed me fruit, never taking a single bite for herself though she could have. We were well off back then because my father was working in Saudi Arabia and even the crates of booze he brought home during his vacations couldn't dent our standard of living. My parents had bought a television, so their friends and our relatives were always over with their children. I can remember my mother making sandwiches for all the children who were absorbed in what they were watching and preparing a light dinner or cake for the adults.

Auntie Saadeya eventually found love when a taxi driver, who was impressed that she'd ignored his flirtatious harassment one day, came to ask my parents for her hand. She'd fallen out with her own family back in the village years ago before moving to Cairo. She hadn't set out to work as a housekeeper, but being illiterate, she lacked other options.

She was told that she wouldn't be a maid because the family was looking for a nanny for their four-year-old daughter and that they'd treat her like she was one of their own. The girl's mother was described as a kind-hearted woman of principle and the father as generous and gentle, so she took a chance, thank God, and in no time at all, she was a member of the family. She even did work around the house, though she wasn't asked to, because she wanted to give Mama a hand. Sometimes, she'd be asked to help in the kitchen on special occasions, but my mother firmly believed that food was at its best when it was made by the lady of the house.

My father insisted that Saadeya have "the full trousseau!" He bought all the household appliances she needed, plus a wedding dress, in Saudi Arabia and then had them shipped to Cairo. We gathered as a family to celebrate Saadeya's upcoming marriage over dinner, and I sang an Umm Kulthum song for her as a wedding present. The grown-ups were very impressed that I'd learned to sing a song like that before I'd even turned six. Uncle Ali may have taken Saadeya away from me, but he was a nice guy and I liked him. When he was courting her, he used to bring me chocolate and he'd take us out on trips in his cab. He was a big reader, and he loved dropping English words into his sentences, but his pronunciation was atrocious. It made my mother giggle, but she approved of him wholeheartedly. "He's gentle and he's educated."

When they got married, Auntie Saadeya went to live with Uncle Ali in a rented apartment, and he told her she had to stop working, but he'd still drive her over to the house in his cab from time to time before he went out to work for the day. My mother would give her whatever she could afford while at the same time chastising her for quitting. "The house feels empty without you!" No one was as trustworthy, as clean, as devoted. Auntie Saadeya would display some reluctance before spending the whole day helping my mother, and then later, when Uncle Ali started leaving her at our house for days at a time because they needed the money, even that pretense was dropped.

Saadeya gave birth to a son, who was like my little brother, and a daughter, who was still an infant when

Uncle Ali went to work in Iraq so that he could earn more money for his growing family. Each month, he sent Saadeya money and a cassette tape on which he'd recorded his messages of lonely longing. After a while, he started sending less money less regularly and stopped sending cassette tapes altogether until eventually he just disappeared. Saadeya was in a tight spot, but so were we, so we couldn't take her back. My mother pleaded her case to our relatives who knew Auntie Saadeya well, and at least two families were happy to support her and her young children and help with clothing and food as best they could. Years later when she learned that Uncle Ali had married an Iraqi woman and settled there, it came as a real shock to her and she couldn't stop crying. She cried even as she dared him to show his face in Cairo again, but Uncle Ali decided to play it safe, returning only when his children were grown and he himself was an old man. The support that the two families provided wasn't enough to keep Saadeya afloat during those difficult years, so she had to work for other clients—some generous, some tight-fisted—whom she told us all about. We also heard about the rheumatoid arthritis and the kidney problems that she got from wearing damp clothes throughout the winter.

The collapse of her marriage changed her, but she never asked for a divorce, not even after she and her children cut costs by moving out of their apartment into a single room with a reed roof in Ain Shams so that she could be closer to her clients, who lived in Heliopolis. On her way to and from the shared bathroom, her neighbors' husbands would try to get her attention, and while their wives certainly made her pay for that, they weren't cruel to her. They understood that she was an "honest woman who minded her own business and that the only thing she cared about was looking after her children." It helped that she'd started praying regularly, dressing in loose galabiyyas, and covering her face when she went out. She locked her children in the room when she went to work and would lock herself in there with them when she got back home. If it hadn't been for the shared bathroom, no one would have ever seen her.

As Mama's illness progressed, Auntie Saadeya's visits started to get on her nerves. She complained that she got headaches from the incessant monologues on pointless topics, including gossip about her clients, but I knew that wasn't the real issue. "She didn't even wash the cup she drank her tea in. She leaves it for me to do."

"She spends the whole week cleaning, Mama. She's exhausted."

"Did I ever say I wanted her to clean the whole house? There's just two plates in the sink; it wouldn't take her a minute." I went to wash the dishes myself as my mother grumbled in the background. "I don't want anyone to visit me anymore! I'm sick and I have enough to worry about already." She knew how much I loved Auntie Saadeya, though, so that was as far as she'd go before changing the subject.

One time Saadeya came to visit while my mother was deciding whether to undergo a risky surgery, and when I got home, I found dishes in the sink and my old nanny's cup of tea on the table still. I figured that my mother had left them for me to do as the customary fine for letting her visit, but before I could start on the dishes, Mama asked me to sit down, appearing both perturbed and tickled in equal measure. "That woman is nuts. She told me that they could come do the surgery for only seven thousand pounds." I asked her in befuddlement who would come do the surgery, but she carried on as though she hadn't heard me. "A shaykh and a genie! Can you believe it? She said they'd come over when I'm all alone in the house with the lights off and that I wouldn't even feel a thing. They'd be gone before I knew it, and then, I'd be totally cured."

"See?" Mama gestured dramatically with one hand. "Didn't I tell you I already had enough to worry about? Now I'm being made to listen to a complete idiot. She was talking about shaykhs and genies!" The story made me laugh, but something weighed on my heart, and when I went to bed that night, I left the light on in the living room. As I lay there thinking about the nameless demon growing inside my mother's chest, I heard a knock at the door, just as I'd been hoping. "Can I sleep beside you tonight, darling?" She asked shyly, but that was exactly what I wanted, too. I held her tightly, my head resting on her chest, as we both drifted off. We'd left the living room lit up overnight for the first time in our lives.

36

A visit to one of the well-known doctors at the Cancer Hospital settled the chemotherapy question. We only went there one time because we quickly realized that the Arab Contractors' Hospital was luxurious in comparison. We spent an entire day there in a crowd of other patients; it was a nightmare. At one point, a doctor and his students encircled my mother, who was sitting slumped over in a wheelchair in the waiting room, muttering Quran verses to herself in all likelihood, and began discussing "the patient's case" in front of everyone. I pushed my way into the middle of the circle to rescue my mother and get her back to Ra'ifa's car as quickly as I could.

While we were there, I'd managed to meet another doctor whose clinic was only a few tram stops away from where we lived. Three doctors at the Cancer Hospital had evaluated my mother's case. Two had said that there was nothing that could be done; one of them was the one who had the clinic nearby. The third was the one who had tried to use her as an example for his students.

I went to the clinic that same evening and waited in the lobby for the doctor to arrive. When he got there, I told him that I'd been at the Cancer Hospital earlier in the day with my mother, and he remembered us, but when I asked him if he'd treat her, he said he was very sorry but he couldn't. I got into the elevator with him and pleaded. By the time we got to the fourth floor, I was begging: "Please treat her, Doctor. I'm begging you." He finally gave in, but only under one condition.

"I'll treat her, but I'm not making any promises." I couldn't have been happier, and after scheduling an appointment for her first round of treatment, I went home to tell my mother the good news. We decided to put the nightmare of the Cancer Hospital behind us and make a new start, then we spent the rest of the evening watching TV together side by side.

37

I sent Ramzi a message through his wife's family informing him of the latest developments because he was still angry and refused to speak to us, though it made very little difference since he called Mama so infrequently anyway. I'd given him a new figure, which was three times what he'd been paying for the radioactive iodine therapy, but he just sent the old amount, not a penny more. My aunt got her sons together, and the younger one agreed to make up the missing two-thirds from Ramzi's share throughout my mother's treatment. The older son and my aunt said that they'd cover any incidentals.

We still got the doctors' union discount, and our new oncologist was happy to work with the medical team at the Arab Contractors' Hospital, where we got a shared room for my mother to save on expenses—no discussion this time. Mama didn't mind sharing a room because she only had to spend the day there hooked up to an IV; I could take her back home when it was done. The doctor had prescribed an anti-nausea medicine to help with some of the side effects from the chemotherapy, but it cost nearly as much as what Ramzi sent us each month. By economizing carefully, I managed to get it, though. When the money arrived, I bought a single blister pack of pills instead of a whole box, and I only gave her two—one on each of the first two days because she didn't need them after that and I could save them for the next session.

I didn't have enough money to buy the anti-nausea medicine after one of the sessions, so the doctor prescribed a different generic that was cheaper. It was only then that I realized how essential that original medicine was. My mother didn't get any sleep that night, and I resolved never to let that happen again. I made sure to buy the anti-nausea medicine before the chemotherapy sessions, and having been informed by sympathetic nurses that the hospital pharmacy charged more than other places, I started buying all her medicines from a well-known chain instead. I remember being very nervous as I carried the vials of medicine back home, terrified that I would trip and fall and smash them all over the sidewalk, but things went smoothly.

I also learned to change Mama's bandages, which saved us money on nurses. I had a little kit containing scissors, bandages, gauze, and antiseptic, which I used to clean her wound. I no longer experienced the terror I'd felt the first time I tried to change her bandage and noticed some flesh coming up through the wound. When my hand brushed against it, it fell off, so I immediately called the doctor while my whole body shivered. He reassured me that it was just dead flesh and that I needed to remove it whenever I changed the bandage. Her wound was the size of a coin, but it extended deep down like a tunnel, all the way to the bone. I got used to it after a few days, and it made me very happy when the doctor praised my careful wound dressing—"Like a pro!" He said that I'd exceeded his expectations, so I told him that I used to dream of becoming a doctor and that we always held on to our dreams one way or another.

Mama prayed for me the whole time while I was changing her bandages. I did it once a day, except for a few times when I got bored of the task and skipped it with her permission. I felt guilty every time, though, because when I went to change the bandage the following day, I'd see that the dark blood had soaked all the way through to her clothes, and she'd complain to me that the putrid smell had kept her up all night. I promised her that I'd never let it happen again, and it was true that I hardly skipped a day for six months.

But sometimes I got angry, too. One time when we were watching television, I turned to tell her something about the show and saw that she was fast asleep. She said the show was "stupid" and I should just let her sleep, so I said she was being a "drag," which pissed her off, and she kicked me out of her bedroom. As soon as I'd left her, I was filled with compassion. I just wanted my mother back. The woman who was constantly dozing beside me wasn't like my mother at all. Even when I rested my head against her chest like a child and she patted me, I couldn't keep thoughts of the tumor beneath me at bay. I told her I wasn't a baby so I'd have an excuse to pull away, but I think she saw through it, and she never pulled me into her chest again after that.

Our fights never lasted long, and we never gave each other the silent treatment—at least not in those days. By the next morning, everything would be back to normal, our fights quickly forgotten because resentment was a luxury that we couldn't afford. My mother once gave me a galabiyya, which had been a gift from my aunt, as a peace offering. "I think it would look so nice on you," she said, knowing full well that she and I would both have to deal with my aunt's pique when she found out. I was so happy I went to try it on right away.

During the final months of her treatment, a friend of mine gave us a wheelchair and, after a lot of wheedling, I finally got Mama to go out with me to the path near our house. The neighbors were so happy to see her, especially those who hadn't visited because "they couldn't bear to see her like that." She was jubilant on our first time out, but on subsequent walks, she became truculent and uncommunicative. All she did was look down at her clean bandage—she'd lost all her hair by then—and occasionally look up at the world around her in silence. I stopped nagging her to go out on walks after she told me that she didn't want anyone to see her like that. She promised me that we'd go out together as soon as "things got back to normal," and I couldn't help but laugh.

"Back to normal? You want us to go back to the way things were before?"

That made her laugh, too. I promised Mama that I wouldn't make her go out anymore.

38

A few months after his blow-up, Ramzi came back to Cairo for a short visit during my mother's treatment. He stayed with his in-laws either because he wanted to avoid running into my aunt and cousins or because he didn't want to get dragged into our mother's daily care, and when he came over, we interacted coolly. Mama had next to no appetite, so Ramzi would bring her bags of the dietary supplement she needed. The two of them sat together for about an hour before Buthayna called and Ramzi had to leave. She had two sessions of chemotherapy left at that point, so Ramzi gave her a little money and promised he'd be back to visit soon.

After the fifth session, Mama was like a ghost. She couldn't get to the bathroom without her cane, and even the short distances she had to cross within the apartment left her out of breath, so she'd plop down on the nearest chair to gather her strength. She would often call for me to help her move around. In the evenings, I used to sit in a chair across from her bed, reading poems that were the subject of my MA thesis, and in the hospital, I sat beside her for hours writing poems of my own.

Whenever I put a book down, she'd ask me how my research was going. "It's going," I'd answer. One time, I said, "Mama, people like me don't have the luxury of doing a master's degree. I don't know what I was thinking." But she never stopped asking me, and she told me that she'd be there at my thesis defense "even if I have to crawl." I read her some of the poems that I'd written about the hospital. I didn't want to at first because I was worried that she might find them painful, but she insisted. She listened and as I got to the end of each stanza, she'd whisper "Allah" under her breath in amazement, as though the poems had given meaning to her journey, as though she finally knew that I would always have a part of her even after she was gone.

39

Mama fell over one night and wasn't able to get back up, so I called Ra'ifa, who came over immediately with her husband. He was able to lift her, so we took her to the nearest hospital. Ra'ifa had called the cardiologist who was treating her own mother, and he came to meet us there. The doctors were concerned about my mother's heart, so they admitted her, and I was only able to cover the additional expense because Ra'ifa's husband furtively handed me an envelope stuffed with cash.

She wouldn't be able to continue with the chemotherapy. Ramzi came back for a very short visit, and within a few days, the exceedingly tender doctor told me that I should take my mother back home. "It'll be better for both of you," he said.

40

No pills, no chemo, just waiting, but I didn't wait for long. Mama became delirious a few days after I took her back home, and it was relentless. She talked constantly, didn't sleep, screamed and ran to the window: "Fire! Fire!" I had to run after her and call for a neighbor to help me restrain her because she was suddenly incredibly powerful. I tried to calm her down and convince her that there was no fire. That I was standing in front of her, talking to her, and not in flames. I took Mama back to bed and lay her down on a pillow that I rested on my legs, rocking her to sleep like a baby as she cried.

I didn't wait long. She fell into a coma a week later and was gone for two months. Nothing more than a body laid out in front of me while I sat keeping an eye out for death's thieving hand.

41

Why do we write poems? It's because they allow us to outsmart the tiny obstacles that life puts in our way. That was what I told myself when I was trying to rig up a stand for the IV bag. I tied a broom tightly to a small chair and then hung the glucose bag from it. "Like a real Robinson Crusoe!" I said to myself. Mama had no idea what was going on, but I'm not sure I was much better. All I could think about was whether the glucose and saline needed replacing. I'd even stopped looking at her. The only thing that mattered about the body lying in front of me was that the empty IV bags had to be replaced with full ones, on time and with precision. I became an hour-hand. Time, just time. Time searching for meaning in timelessness. Futility given structure by time.

She only woke up twice. Once, screaming—"Your brother's dead!"—and then falling straight back into unconsciousness. The screaming had startled me, but I wasn't shaken by the conclusion that she'd reached because I'd been sure that Ragi was dead for years by that point. She must have been re-living the events of her life. At dawn, I looked through the window in her bedroom and saw a sparrow flitting between branches on the tree outside. Life on the other side of the bedroom wall seemed serene, like there was a rhythm to it, so I sat beside the window the whole time my mother was in a coma.

The second time was shortly before she died. She woke up and called my name, so I ran to her bedside. I simply couldn't believe it. She asked for some water, so I gave it to her, and then I asked, "Have I made you proud, Mama?"

"Of course, my dear," she replied, softly, shutting her eyes again. I called all my girlfriends that day to tell them that my mother knew who I was and that she was proud of me.

I prayed to God that I wouldn't have to watch her die. I got her a new medical mattress that was filled with air because that was better for bed sores, and a friend helped me move her from my grandmother's daybed to my bed, which was next to a window. It was late July and hot. One day while I was changing the bandages on her wound and bed sores, as well as her diaper, I noticed that her abdomen was distended, so I mentioned it to a doctor friend, who said he'd come take a look. When he inserted a catheter, I heard her moan softly, but not in pain; it was relief, like laying down a heavy burden. The bloating went away after that.

I set my alarm clock, attached a new glucose bag to her IV, and checked that the new mattress was doing its job before sitting down next to her and launching into a long conversation. I told her how much I loved her and that I'd never leave her side no matter how long she needed me. I can remember laughing at the end of my speech after I said, "But please don't let it be tomorrow. It's my birthday." It felt like Mama smiled when I said that. I kissed her forehead and lay on a mattress on the floor beside her.

I slept deeply until the morning, having been unable to sleep for two hours in a row for months because whenever I drifted off, I'd leap up again suddenly to check on Mama. I was in a coma of my own that night until I was finally awoken by the power going out. I didn't check on Mama first thing like I always did because the deflating mattress—a whistle of air escaping—had commanded my attention. I tried to stand up, but a whirling black cloud had settled over the room, which suddenly felt cramped as though countless invisible beings were working industriously. When things settled down and I could finally get to my feet, I saw Mama's head, turned away from me, her lips pursed like a flute-player, eyes shut. There was no sign of the spasms she'd felt. She was completely serene. As was I as I looked at her, kissed her forehead, which was still warm, and rested my head against her chest. Mama was dead.

42

A few days earlier, Ramzi had asked me how our mother was doing over the phone, so I told him she was dying, and he promised to come as quickly as possible. During the final month of Mama's illness, I'd hired a young woman to sit with her for a few hours in the daytime so that I could get some rest. After I got off the phone with Ramzi, I told her that I was going to sleep for a few hours, and then I threw myself on the bed. I couldn't feel my body, however. I'd overslept, so the girl came in to tell me that I'd have to pay her more if I wanted her to stay longer. I told her she could go and that I'd handle things myself. Ramzi called again later to say that he was sorry, but he wouldn't be able to come because his visa sponsor had taken away his passport. I knew that was a lie because in all the years that he'd lived in Saudi Arabia, he could always travel when he wanted to.

He didn't call again until the day Mama died after his father-in-law broke the news. I'd just returned home from burying her. "She's gone?" He asked tearfully. "Did you bury her already?" I didn't respond, so he told me that he was going to do a pilgrimage just for her. "Should I get on a plane tomorrow?"

"And what would be the point of that?"

We didn't speak again until he arrived in Cairo a few months later. Buthayna's parents went to pick the family up at the airport and bring them back to the house. I'd cleared my mother's bed out of her bedroom and set up seating for the people who came to give their condolences, and that was where Ramzi and his in-laws gathered to exchange their recent news. After they took the kids to bed, Ramzi and Buthayna went into their bedroom, and I could hear them making love when I went to use the bathroom. I shut the door to my bedroom and rarely left unless I had to.

Buthayna's family were over more and more, and in the evenings, when she and Ramzi would watch television in their bedroom, he'd invite me to join them. I tried one time because a good film was playing, but when I lay down on the bed beside them, he teased me, "You better not fall asleep before the film's over. Buthayna hates that!" I told them that I felt very sleepy all of a sudden and slipped out.

Ramzi never asked me where I'd buried our mother, and he never spoke about her at all. It was like she hadn't been there just a few months ago. He once came into my bedroom and caught sight of a bottle of alcohol beside my bed, but he didn't deliver the sermon that I was expecting. "I'm worried about your health," was what he said.

They stayed for more than a month. When my friends came over, we'd sit in my bedroom, but my aunt refused to step foot in the house so long as Ramzi was there. Her daughter, on the other hand, called Ramzi to ask him how long he'd be in town, but she was surprised to receive a cold reaction since he'd never been hostile to her in the past. She was the one who told me he'd be leaving in a couple of days, so I left my bedroom door open the following day in case he wanted to stick his head in and talk, but he kept his shut, and when I woke up the next morning, they were gone.

43

Friends don't believe me when I tell them that I'm thinking about selling my house so that I can buy a grave. The only reason I bought a big house was so that I could sell it one day if I got sick so that I wouldn't have to depend on anyone. The thought of death keeps me up at night more than anything that has to do with life. Burying my mother next to her mother was far more difficult than I expected. Mama hadn't been in contact with her family for ages—so long that the young relative who was responsible for the family tomb initially refused to bury her there because he'd never met her.

I'd done so many things in preparation for her death. Following a friend's advice, I put the money for her shroud, burial, and funeral along with the money left over from her medical expenses into a bag that I set aside. My friends had written out a post-mortem to-do list for me so I had a script to follow. The list told me who to call first to get the burial certified, then to call a guy who would take care of the burial permit, and then the woman who would wash my mother's body. I was like a robot when she died, following every instruction precisely, but I still didn't know where I was going to bury her up until a few days before her foreseeable death.

I declined Ra'ifa's husband's invitation to bury my mother in his plot, a recent purchase, when he explained that it was an in-ground burial, one where she'd be covered by dirt. I asked my cousin about their family tomb where my father was buried, but she said that it had been leveled to build a tall building. My aunt's eldest son wasn't very excited about the idea of burying my mother in their new family tomb because he thought his own mother wasn't very long for this world. I implored my aunt to intervene with the family urgently because I knew she was still close to a few of them whom she saw often and with whom she felt a connection rooted in the distant past. She called one of the family elders, who agreed to bury Mama in the family tomb while cautioning the rest of us that there was absolutely no room for any future deceased because the tomb was packed.

I was so happy when the family agreed and the sight of the tomb filled me with pride. It was made of elegant marble, decorated with fine calligraphy, and surrounded by vibrant flowers. "Where are her kids?" the gravedigger shouted.

"Me, I'm her daughter," I said as I leaned on a friend for support. He looked past me.

"No, ladies don't go down into the crypt." Two men in the crowd picked up Mama's body and carried it down into the crypt behind the gravedigger. I felt such relief. I'd heard the exact same thing from her when I'd told her before she died that I didn't want to carry her into the crypt myself: "Women don't go down into the crypt."

That was 1994. I turned thirty-six years old the day my mother died. I said goodbye to her there that day, and I haven't been back to see her since. The excuse I make is that my mother herself thought that visiting graves was a waste of time. Occasionally, I get the desire to go looking for her grave, but mostly all I do is just recite the opening chapter of the Quran and pray for mercy whenever I drive by the area, struggling to remember precisely where I left her.

44

My brother was always telling me that he "got in the way of his wife's career." I never knew if he was saying it for my benefit or if he really believed it. Ever since Mama died, I'd stopped trying to figure out how much of what Ramzi was saying was true. Now every time he smiled, I worried that he was going to ask me for something.

Ramzi and Buthayna got engaged when she was still in high school, so he used to stay up late writing out cheat sheets for her in his tidy minute handwriting before explaining to her what to do so that she wouldn't get caught by the proctors. That always gave them the giggles. He once spent an entire night looking for her runaway cat because she said that she wouldn't go to her exam the following day unless her cat came back. Whenever he asked her to do something, she always asked the same question—"How Much Are You Gonna Give Me?"—which had some euphoric effect on him. He always praised her money smarts and said she could out-negotiate him. When she got admitted to the philosophy department at Cairo University, he carried on making cheat sheets for her until he got offered a job in Saudi Arabia. For a year or two, she flew back for her exams, but eventually she gave it up.

Ramzi loved to draw when he was a kid, and the whole family was obsessed with his sketchbook. He and his friends used to make the news poster for me when I was in elementary school, and mine was always the prettiest one by far. He always included a new element with each iteration, and the way he sprayed the paint made the surface look like magic. I spent so much time just sitting beside him in awe as he decorated them. I loved telling the teachers that the artist was "MY BIG BROTHER" when they asked.

After I graduated, he told me the same thing about "getting in the way of Buthayna's career," and then he said, "We were talking and she might go back to university to study in the Arabic Department just like you." I hadn't expected her to pick Arabic, and I'd certainly thought that she'd given up on her degree a long time ago, but I wasn't completely taken aback. The more gold she wore around her neck and wrists, the more the career thing seemed like a joke, but I pretended to be sympathetic. I told him that studying Arabic wasn't as easy as he might have thought, but I was happy to help Buthayna with her application and tutor her during her degree if that was what they wanted. He accepted my offer enthusiastically, but when he came back a few days later, he laughingly told me that he thought Buthayna was a hundred percent right when she said that our family was "a bunch of lunatics."

That was the last I heard of it for a while—until I finished my master's degree after our mother died. Buthayna's brother had recently been hired as a flight attendant, and that prompted Ramzi to turn to me and say, "Don't you wish you were still a flight attendant? You'd have a little fortune saved up."

"You do know that I'm writing a PhD thesis, right?"

"What difference does that make? You could've done both at the same time." When I said nothing in response, he realized that he wasn't making any sense and quickly changed the subject as he slipped the photo I'd given him of me in my graduation robes into his pocket.

45

My mother died on my birthday, which I took as a sign of re-birth, and it left me feeling liberated, not sad—at least at first. At the funeral, the Quran-reciter had to tell me and my friends off a few times for laughing too loud. After everyone left, I went to bed, but I kept waking up every two hours to change the glucose bag, and I had to remind myself that my mother was dead and my duties were over. It took me an entire month before I started sleeping through the night without interruption—before I understood deep-down that she was gone.

46

I almost missed my flight to Tunis because I overslept. One of my friends was calling to wake me up, but I didn't even hear the phone beside me ringing until it was already quite late, so I got up in a hurry, and thankfully I managed to catch my flight at the very last second. I hadn't slept deeply like that for a long time, and I wasn't used to it, but the trip to Tunis a month after my mother's death was a godsend.

On the flight there, I sat beside the other poet—also an Arab woman—whom I'd be speaking with at the event, and we got to talking. When she asked me if I'd come to terms with my mother's death, I didn't know how to answer the question, so she rephrased it more directly: "Have you made peace with the fact that the only way you'll ever get to see her again is through a photo?"

I had such a great time on that trip. I laughed a lot and went out at night, danced, and drained one glass of delicious Tunisian wine after the other. The poet stuck by me the entire trip, even when I was directionless, and as I fastened my seat belt on the flight back, it felt like I was experiencing everything for the first time.

When I got back, the house was empty and all I could do was throw myself onto the ground in the exact spot where Mama had died. I cried so much I thought I'd never stop.

47

My neighbor and I used to refer to the building as Ahmad Wahby's house. She'd moved in as a young bride about four years after us with her husband, who'd just come back from Hungary with a doctorate in geology. The house was a one-story building divided into two apartments; we lived in one of them, and the landlord, who was from a large and well-known rural family, had lived in the other before he decided to rent it out to the young couple. He wasn't married himself, and despite working for a prominent judge, had never finished his law degree.

Our landlord built the unremarkable house in the deserts of Heliopolis. At the time, the only other buildings in the area were a two-story building across the street, which was owned by a brigadier-general and would later be replaced by a high-rise with shops on the ground floor, and a five-story building at the end of the street where my friend Ra'ifa lived on the second floor. She and I used to signal to each other from our respective balconies before I'd get dressed and go over to her place, where we talked and shared secrets—a routine that has stayed the same since I was eighteen years old despite changes of address and destiny.

Mama and I could see my father and brothers getting off the tram from more than a kilometer away because there was nothing to block our view. The area was full of stray dogs, but they all obeyed Ramzi. He could tame anything—even rats, which he kept in the bathtub. They would come running to him in the evenings for food.

Over time, we became friends with our landlord–neighbor Mr. Ahmad, who was grateful that we looked the other way when he snuck women into his apartment. We sat up on the roof together on summer evenings like one big family, enjoying the delicacies he brought back from the countryside: grapes, flaky pastry, honey, and aged cheese.

Mr. Ahmad loved helping people, and he never said no to a favor unless you wanted to borrow money or were late on your rent. He used to ride the metro for free with his student ID card, and he thought that anyone who took taxis—even when it was absolutely necessary—was "nuts." In the winter, he wore the same suit over and over, and in summer, he dressed in threadbare pants and a faded t-shirt that he'd brought back from Libya.

I can't remember my mother or anyone else in the family going to a government office without him, though. He knew how to cut through bureaucracy—his important employer helped—and he could get things done in a single day that would normally take months. It was his only form of generosity, but it was enough, and we were all very grateful.

He eventually moved out to a rented apartment owned by one of his siblings near Ibn Sandar Square. Family members died and their heirs inherited, but Mr. Ahmad's situation stayed exactly the same, as did his complaints: his nephew's mistreatment—barging in on him in their shared apartment unannounced—and his lack of funds.

Once a year, he'd turn up at the house in his old suit, clean shirt, and tie, carrying a Samsonite briefcase, and he'd tell us that he wanted to sell the building so that he could get on with his life and get married like everyone else had, but he always asked for a ridiculous price that sent buyers running.

The plan was always soon abandoned, Mr. Ahmad returning to his normal life and my mother, the neighbor, and I all sharing a laugh. "Here we go again," we'd whisper to one another when he returned with his annual enthusiasm.

As desert became city, the house stood out more and more, looking like a village elder's house, while around it upmarket high-rises popped up, blocking our view of the tram stop and the sun. We had to stop sitting on the roof because people could watch us from above. That didn't stop the landlord from turning up each month to collect the miniscule rent and our carefully apportioned share of the water bill before sitting down beside Mama's bed and conversing with her about life's hardships.

48

I was sitting on the balcony when I spotted him on the other side of the railing looking back at me, and when I gave him a big hug, he started crying like a baby, so I patted his head, but I didn't cry myself. We went into the house, where I made him a cup of tea, and I could see he was overcome with joy. He called Buthayna right away and told her to get the girls ready to come see their aunt. They all came over to the house at least once or twice, and as they were heading back to Saudi Arabia, he asked me to check in on his eldest daughter, who would be living with her grandparents while she attended university.

I ignored his hints that she'd be much better off staying with me because it was easy to pretend that I hadn't picked up on them. I was working on my doctoral thesis at the time, and I'd got used to living alone, so the responsibility of looking after a young woman was something I could neither handle nor stomach.

My niece came to visit me a lot, and we soon became friends, spending entire days together, eating the nice meals she prepared. I allowed her to invite friends over, and when they were there, the house was full and boisterous, but always within reasonable limits. When her younger sister moved back to Cairo to start university herself, it felt like I had a family again. Buthayna's parents' apartment was too small, so Ramzi bought a big, fancy apartment nearby, and his other two daughters moved in with their sisters and grandparents as well. He also purchased a car for the eldest, who became responsible for taking her sisters back and forth to school and university, and even though Ramzi and Buthayna remained in Saudi Arabia, they spoke to their daughters by phone throughout the day. The girls visited less frequently, eventually stopping altogether, and when I went to see them at their apartment, Buthayna's parents made me feel like a guest, which I couldn't stand. I only went over when Ramzi and Buthayna were in town—once or twice per trip—since they came back to Cairo all the time then.

49

The only thing Ramzi knew about me was that I was close to finishing my PhD and that I'd finally got a job teaching at a provincial university. One day flipping the channels as he ironed his clothes, he happened upon a TV interview I'd given about my career as a poet, so he called to his wife and daughters to come see "their aunt on TV!" as he later recounted to me in astonishment.

When I went to visit him at his glitzy apartment, Buthayna would go to call on her parents, giving us privacy. She finally trusted us, both me and him. We would sit side by side watching television together in silence or he'd tell me about his new plans for the cream business and all the money he was raking in. I always pretended to be interested in what he was saying, so one time I suggested that he start selling his creams in Egypt. "Each one goes for four hundred riyals. How much do you think I can get for them here? Are you stupid or something?" Once when Buthayna was out, he asked me how I was doing, and I was in so much debt at the time that I opened up to him while trying to sound as if I wasn't worried about anything. "Oh, I am too. Everyone's up to their eyeballs in debt these days," he said. I never bothered again after that. I never spoke to him about the problems I faced, and all he ever did was make small talk even when his wife was out.

50

Ra'ifa has been asking me when I'm going to finish this book a lot recently. She even accuses me of being lazy from time to time. "It isn't easy to bare your life like this!"

"People need to know what you've been through. How you got here. It hasn't been easy." I admire her audacity, but I don't know how to explain to her that no matter how we've lived, when it comes to broadcasting our stories like this, we're all cowards. She once asked me bashfully if I had mentioned her in the book, so I told her that I wrote about the part she played when Mama was sick. "The part I played? Do you think we were acting?" she asked, gesticulating grandly, before her face suddenly darkened. "Don't forget your mother asked me to look after you before she died." I hadn't.

Right before she went into a coma, during the time when she didn't want to see anyone at all, Mama asked me to invite Ra'ifa over, and when she arrived, she asked me to give them some privacy. "I told her never to leave your side no matter what happens," Mama later told me. After she died, Ra'ifa's family spoiled me as if I were one of them. They put up with me—all of them, big and small—when I was angry, anxious, happy; it didn't matter. I was like a fallen tree branch they'd planted in their family garden, and as I took root over time, they forgot that I hadn't always been there.

Mama treated Ra'ifa like a second daughter, and they became friends by virtue of being neighbors until she decided that Ra'ifa and I were better suited. "You're closer to her age. You two should be friends." She was happy to see her "two daughters" grow so close.

Ra'ifa brings up the miracle of my mother's shrouded corpse whenever I see her, but I'm fairly certain that she imagined the whole thing and the skepticism always shows on my face. My memory of that day is partial at best. I remember standing in the bedroom with the woman who'd come to wash Mama's body before the burial, and all I could smell was cheap, cloying perfume. Who decided to spray that instead of using my mother's favorite 555 Cologne, which she had lined up beside her bed? The corpse-washer muttered some phrases, and then addressing Mama directly, she spoke sternly: "So long. God give you strength when you account for your life." It made me sick to watch her just going through the motions. "Is it just you and me? Why don't you see if any of the guests want to help."

I sloshed across the wet floor to open the door and found Ra'ifa on the other side. "She says she needs another pair of hands, folks," I said, avoiding Ra'ifa's gaze because I knew she was terrified of anything having to do with death.

"I'll do it," she said instantly. "I'll help wash Tante Suad." Together, we turned my mother over just as we'd done when she was in a coma. Ra'ifa spoke to Mama non-stop as though she weren't dead and she put the corpse-washer in her place, too. "Hey, be careful. Don't be so rough." We nearly broke out in giggles when she said that, and I thought I saw Mama smile.

According to the legend that Ra'ifa liked to tell, my mother's body had reverted to its youthful form after her death. She said that Mama's skin was glowing and flushed and that she'd never been more beautiful. She was a bride, not a corpse. I never know what to say when she tells the story, so she asks me questions like, "Weren't you there? Don't you remember how beautiful she was?"

"I guess I was thinking about more urgent matters," I plead, and we share a laugh.

I know it wasn't easy for her, though. She did it out of love and loyalty, and she's never done it again since, not even when her sisters died. "To be honest with you, that was the first and last time I'll ever wash a corpse. It took me months to stop trembling afterward." I knew what she meant because I, too, had felt uneasy for months after washing my aunt's corpse, according to her wishes, and I swore that I'd never do it again. I went back on my oath later, however.

I haven't written much about Ra'ifa in this book even though she's been a big part of my life for the past forty years, but I know she doesn't mind because she's not the type to conceal her displeasure. "I don't understand the stuff you write, to be honest, but I do feel it," she'll say to me, smirking. I try not to give her too much poetry to read, though, because I can remember how Mama used to complain that she didn't understand what I was trying to say. You should write a whole book about Ra'ifa, I tell myself, but I know I won't get around to it. I don't know how to explain to her that everyone I've written about here is dead. I've chosen to write about them because they're dead. Some of them are actually dead while others are just dead to me. How do you explain a very basic truth to someone who lives inside your own heart? How do you explain that the reason you want to write about distant roots is so that they'll float up into the air like a flurry of leaves and never be fooled into thinking they were once a tree. I'm describing a rotten stump in order to get rid of it. In order to separate myself from it before I die. I don't want to get used to it. I don't want to lose the ability to distinguish its fetid odor from the fragrance of life. How can I explain a basic truth like that to Ra'ifa, who adores her family, when to me, nothing could be more obvious. How do I get her to understand what poetry has taught me: writing is another death. I haven't written about Ra'ifa because I don't want her to die.

51

Ramzi decided that he wasn't going to take any of our old furniture to the new apartment. I watched him as he scanned each piece one after the other, reconsidering his decision, but he didn't waver. The furniture in our apartment was almost twenty years old, and I was constantly having to glue legs and arms back onto chairs as they fell off. He bought me a new stove (on installment) after he saw me light the old one, flames shooting up from the only functioning burner toward my face. "That thing's a fire hazard!" He couldn't help but mention that he'd bought the stove in Buthayna's name because she'd be the one making the payments, or so he claimed. As they were leaving, he joked with me that since his wife and daughters were the ones with their names on the deed of the new place, he might have to move back in with me if they kicked him out. I didn't laugh at his joke, and I couldn't think of anything to say either. Everything around me was unsettling. I wasn't making progress with my PhD thesis, the university was pressuring me to finish, and my debts were piling up because all I had to live on was my meager salary. I no longer had access to my father's pension and I couldn't take on another job.

A while later, Ramzi invited me to spend a few days with them at their new beach house in a resort called Stella di Mare, but I made an excuse about having too much work on my hands.

Life was good, though, all the same. Throughout my life, I'd kept my relatives at bay, but over time, my aunt's daughter and I became good friends, and of course, I'd also grown close to her brother who'd essentially paid for all my mother's care in the final months after she started chemotherapy. He continued to send me money every month so that I could focus on my PhD, and the generous cash gifts he gave me on holidays went some way to paying off my debts. I was planning to finish my PhD thesis within the next year, which would earn me a promotion and a salary bump.

As a reward for finishing my MA—with distinction—my aunt's daughter helped me knock down the wall between Mama's bedroom and the front room overlooking the street. There was some back-and-forth with the landlord, but I finally had a living room with a balcony and two large windows. I got a cat, who promptly ran away to find a mate, and I turned the dining room table into an agreeable desk.

Ramzi and his family would come to visit when he was in town and I, too, would go to see them at their house on rare occasions, but the visits never lasted very long. We didn't speak about Mama after she died. It was as if she'd never existed. I used to visit my aunt from time to time, although not because Mama was dead—it was more that I felt tremendous gratitude toward her. Her views about me hadn't changed: I was "spoiled," but she praised me for having cared for my mother and for my academic success, "which no one saw coming," she liked to tell me. But I was still spoiled. All the same, she never tried to mother me. As she grew older, she became a child herself, and all she wanted was to be coddled. A few days before she died, she looked up at me coyly and asked me to wash her body as I'd done for my mother, so I did.

How many times has someone warned me that I was "heading for the rocks?" A lot. It feels like the current's been pushing me toward those rocks my entire life. At times, I bob on the surface like a cork; at others, I sink. I was floating carelessly on my back, I tell my friends, before his return had me swimming hard against the surging current.

The Lost One Returns as the Curtain Begins to Rise!

1

HOW LONG HAD IT BEEN since Mama died? I didn't normally think about it, but one morning, I got a jubilant phone call from our old friend in Germany who told me that he'd found Ragi. Though it had actually been Ragi who found the friend at home when he called from a church that helped irregular migrants return to their countries of origin without facing any punishment.

I'd been certain that he was dead. Mama had even woken up from the coma once to scream it. I was sad to learn that her coma experience hadn't been as sacred as I'd thought, and that the visions she'd seen were just ordinary dreams. I'd been trying to make sense of visions for my entire life because the act of interpreting sustained me, but the coma wasn't the rite I'd taken it for as I kept vigil by her bedside. I thought it was a once-in-a-lifetime experience, although it did happen to some people more than once, but the first time was always the most intense and excruciating, just like love. The news called into question everything I'd been told: that the comatose can hear us when we speak, that the things we say reassure them and pull them back toward life. That was all bullshit. Nothing like that had happened. Mama was sleeping, and she'd had a nightmare just like anybody who eats a heavy meal before bed. Perhaps the life she'd lived had given her indigestion. Life is a cliché like that. It doesn't care about our fears or needs, our ceaseless struggle to yank our loved ones back from the precipice. All we can do in this capsized life is grieve without end, direction, or feeling.

I was elated nonetheless. I pranced around the house singing the song my mother had listened to most in her final days:

When I heard, "It's a boy!"
My heart filled with joy.

That evening, I got a call from Ragi, who'd been told by our mutual friend that his mother was dead and that his sister was happy to hear that he was still alive. It was the first time I'd ever heard him cry. It felt a bit strange consoling him since I'd stopped grieving for Mama a long time ago. I wasn't the type to wallow; at least not back in those days, when I was racing against time. I was trying to finish my long-overdue PhD thesis under threats of termination, so self-pity was a luxury I couldn't afford.

I remembered the promise I'd made to her before she lost consciousness: "I swear to God I'll go looking for him, if I can afford to." But I could never afford to. About a year before he turned up, I got invited to a poetry festival in Germany for a few days, but I didn't go looking for him when I was there even though the thought had occurred to me. I couldn't help but laugh when I imagined myself turning my back on the audience and walking out of the festival to roam the streets of Frankfurt in search of a brother I hadn't seen for more than thirty years.

Even Ramzi was in high spirits. He was back in Cairo on one of his frequent trips to check in on his daughters when Ragi made contact, so he and Buthayna came over to talk things through. He told me that Ragi had also called him in tears, and he seemed genuinely moved. Then he asked me how I was feeling about the situation, so I said that I thought Ragi should come back home as soon as possible. Ramzi agreed that that was the only option, but he got lost in thought for a moment before adding, "I think I might set him up with a small business and rent a little apartment for him because I don't think you'll be able to stand having him here." My view was that the most pressing thing was to get Ragi back to his mother's house as quickly as possible and then see how things turned out. We could always explore other options if I found I couldn't cope. Ramzi agreed.

Ragi couldn't come back to Egypt until he'd paid a fine for failing to complete his military service, so Ramzi paid it and then promptly made a fuss about the cost of the plane ticket, but Ragi assured him that the church would pay for his flight, and that settled the matter. I began making preparations for his arrival.

I honestly had no objection to having Ragi back home again. I'd been living on my own since Mama died, and I was forty-five years old. My brother's return seemed like an occasion for hope and conviviality.

Where would he sleep? The renovations had left the apartment with only one bedroom, so I had to make the best of it. I hung a curtain where the wall we'd knocked down used to be, separating the room at the front—Ragi's old bedroom—from the room where our mother had slept and died. I wanted it to resemble his old bedroom but to have its own unique energy. He could pull the curtain back to let Mama's soul in, to let her embrace him and look after him. That was still the way I saw things despite my recent confrontation with the truth about comas.

I filled the refrigerator with all the foods he liked, though I really had to trawl my memory: Roquefort, basterma, cold cuts. Smiling to myself, I hid the white cheese behind some plastic containers because he always used to complain when Mama set it on the table. He called it 'Cockroaches!'

"White cheese again? We have it every day!" He used to say. I filled the refrigerator with beer bottles, too.

Ramzi had already left for Saudi Arabia by the time Ragi finished his paperwork and got on a plane to Cairo, so my oldest niece drove me to the airport to pick him up. I was worried that I wouldn't recognize him, but I rejected her suggestion of a sign with his name on it. "A sign? What are you talking about? There's no way I won't recognize my own brother!" She didn't say anything, but I could see the dejection on her face. It was the same face she gave me whenever I asked her to fix something on the computer.

"There's no fixing it, Auntie! You have to get a new one."

She was spared a lecture this time, however. I was too busy scanning the faces of passengers as they walked out of the arrivals hall, worried that I'd miss him.

In the end, I recognized Ragi right away from the look in his eyes as he searched through the waiting crowd. He seemed gaunt and shorter, dressed in a faded t-shirt and old jeans. I could see the disappointment on my niece's face when she saw the state of her uncle who'd just flown in from Germany. When he got closer, I shouted his name and he turned toward me, smiling, and gave me a hug. All he had with him was a carry-on bag slung over his shoulder, and I noticed a thick black leather cuff around one of his wrists; it looked like the kind of armbands that thugs wore, but I later learned that he wore it for the arthritis he'd developed from working in kitchens for many years. I felt for him.

When we got home, it was just the two of us; our niece had used the excuse of homework to make a quick exit. Ragi said he wasn't hungry, and it seemed obvious to me that the things I'd remembered him liking in the distant past were no longer to his taste. He declined a tour of the renovated apartment. He just asked me where the bathroom was, and when he came out, he went into his bag to retrieve a German-Arabic dictionary, which he began flipping through. No matter what I said, his only response was peevish laughter.

He enjoyed the beer I'd got, though, and drank one bottle after another. At one point, he decided to show me the contents of his wallet. The church had given him two hundred euros, and he was planning to write to friends in Germany when he got settled to borrow even more.

When Ramzi and Buthayna returned to Cairo a couple of weeks later, I could tell that he was going to go back on his promise. He called in the afternoon to let me know that they'd arrived but that he wouldn't be able to come by the house until the following morning because he was exhausted from the trip. There was zero enthusiasm in his voice, so I could sense that something was up. Ramzi was never fake with me, and I could predict what he was going to do just from the tone of his voice.

He and Buthayna came over the next morning, and after kisses and hugs were exchanged, he asked Ragi, "So what are your plans?" Ragi said that he wanted to discuss the business project that Ramzi had mentioned and then he got up to take some papers out of his bag. Ramzi was shocked that Ragi had already started crunching numbers, and he quickly caught Buthayna's eye before asking, "Business? When did I say anything about opening a business?" He had the innocent act down cold.

Later that night, Ragi swore to me that Ramzi had said they'd go into business together; he even showed me the feasibility study that he'd prepared. I couldn't make sense of any of the diagrams or numbers, but I tried to act interested to assuage his anger. Of course, I believed him. I'd seen the look on Ramzi's face. It was the same look he'd given me when we were at the hospital together. I felt a twinge when I remembered him saying, "There's no way I can pay for the chemotherapy. I just can't, I'm sorry."

2

Ragi slowly settled in, and as his Arabic improved, I learned that he'd worked as a cook the whole time he was away. He promised he'd take responsibility for feeding me so that I could focus on my thesis. He regaled me with stories about the fantastical life he'd led, spending money left and right, but when I tried to bring up his twenty years of silence, he changed the subject by spinning more yarns and comparing the furniture in his apartment in Germany to the shabby furniture that surrounded us. He could talk for hours without taking a break as he used to do with Mama.

He would set a stopwatch when he was cooking to make sure that the meal was served on time and to show me how precise he was—how precise German life was. I once suggested that he could prepare food for people we knew for extra money so that he wouldn't have to depend on Ramzi, but he made excuses about his bad back and then spent the whole of the next day in bed, saying that he'd "aggravated it."

He used to hang up on my friends if they called at mealtimes, but it was only later when they would recount those incidents, laughing, that I understood that they had suppressed any offense they'd felt for my sake and for the sake of my "German" brother who had strong opinions about when it was appropriate to call a person at home.

I wasn't allowed to be a minute late. I would run through the house, tossing whatever book I had in my hand aside, to get to my seat at the dining table, which Ragi had set very carefully. It was just like his "fits of enthusiasm" when we were younger when he'd insist that the whole family sit down together at the dining table for a meal at a specified time. At first, I tried to act out the lines from *Zizi's Family*, which had been such a boon to me in the past, but they no longer made us laugh. Day after day, the jokes crashed ever harder, but the comedienne, who made a point of ignoring the audience's grim expression, never tired of repeating them.

I'd given up my habit of watching black-and-white Egyptian films after dinner to clear my head when Ragi moved back in. Instead, we talked for hours. I would start, but by the third sentence, he'd have already taken over the conversation, and nothing could shut him up after that. The only time he actually listened was when I told stories about Mama, though they would quickly lead to a vicious argument because he always had to interrupt me to criticize her for "ruining things as usual."

Tears filled his eyes whenever he asked me about her illness. I always described it as though it was the first time he was hearing it, as though I were re-living it. I hadn't spoken about it in many years—not with my close friends who'd been at my side through it all and not with the friends I'd made since who asked because they wanted to "get to know me better." My friends and I eventually stopped talking about Mama's illness because we had other things going on in our lives and because the story was mine. Every detail belonged to me. I could tell it—including the ending—whenever I wanted. I knew that I'd never forget it. I kept it framed and stored in my heart.

But Ragi wanted to hear the story every night. He knew how to poke at it to get it to bleed. It was like he wanted to root himself to the house where he'd only lived for two short years before moving to Germany, and the story of our mother's demise was the only way to do that. I guess I wanted to release it, to tell the story until I was sobbing, until fear had seized me, but I was scared that there'd be a price to pay for telling the story over and over again to satisfy him. That the frame would crack and the story would vanish.

Ragi couldn't resist getting me to tell the story each night over our obligatory dinner, and he was always waiting for a chance to interrupt—to complain about how Mama had "coddled" him and how the coddling had caused him to suffer for years. The two stories seemed to be intertwined, so they had to be told simultaneously. As my energy flagged, Ragi appeared victorious, talking for hours and hours about people I didn't know, cities I'd never visited, a language I didn't understand. It made him angry when I failed to laugh on cue, so he'd change the subject and start talking about our father, which was when I'd lose interest completely—especially when he'd say the same thing that Ramzi always did: "You just didn't know Dad."

Over time, I discovered that I didn't know any of them. Not even our mother, whom Ragi spoke about with such uncommon anger. She was someone else. Ragi's stories made me feel vulnerable, as though I would be the next victim of his opinions and disgust. I couldn't understand where the cruelty came from, and I was worried that my treasured memories would be transformed into a forest of images I could only walk through alone.

In the mornings, he'd ask where our mother was buried—never once asking about our father—because he wanted to go visit her and he wanted me to go with him. "We have a duty," he'd say. Mama had been dead for more than a decade when I started seeing her face when I looked in the mirror sometimes. By the time Ragi came back, the resemblance was obvious, at least to me, and after I'd listen to him rant for hours, I'd escape to my bedroom and bury my head in my hands just as she once did.

3

His bedroom was full of scraps of paper on which he wrote everything—every move he made—while he listened to music, but not as loudly as before since I asked him to wear headphones so that I could study in peace. He used to wake up early to go out shopping. The two hundred euros were long gone and his German friends had all expressed "regret" that they were unable to lend him any money. Gone, too, was the small amount that Ramzi had given him to help cover expenses, so he started borrowing money from me, coming and going in great excitement. There was always something he'd forgotten to buy, so he'd have to scurry back out again. In the evenings, he brought me scraps of paper on which he'd diligently recorded the money he owed and swore that he'd pay it all back as soon as he found a job.

For my part, I carried copies of Ragi's CV with me wherever I went. I pored through old address books and went to see relatives whom I never imagined visiting. I even went to visit my uncle's children whom I hadn't seen in years because of the way I felt toward their parents. I could never get past it and I didn't see why I should.

My cousins welcomed me warmly, and they were very sympathetic about the "pickle" I'd found myself in; they liked the new me. I hadn't gone over to defy them as I had my uncle years ago—"But, Uncle, I'm a poet," I'd said in my faraway youth—because I'd already made a life for myself in poetry. To them, I seemed stronger than I'd been in the past, and as parents for whom their children's education was paramount, it mattered to them that I was a university lecturer who was about to earn a PhD. I accepted their help gratefully. They helped to get Ragi two rare job opportunities at a large hotel, which he promptly squandered, one after the other, in a matter of days. He expressed no regret and made no apologies—not to me, or to them.

4

My poet friend who lives abroad and speaks German well met Ragi when she came over to the house one day and she told me she thought he might have been in prison during the time he'd broken off contact with us. He was delighted that she spoke to him in German at first, but his demeanor changed shortly after they began talking, and he soon walked out of the room, frowning, and refrained from buzzing around the house as he normally did while she was over. The thought pained me, but it was the alibi I'd been looking for. It was like my friend had given me a magical formula for rationalizing everything Ragi had put me through. It made me pity him at least; helped me accept my fate. As I was about to turn fifty, I'd become a mother to a man who was nearly sixty himself. When I confronted Ragi and told him that I just wanted to know the truth—that I didn't care what he'd done, I'd never be ashamed of him and would always support him—he looked at me contemptuously. "Prison? That's nonsense. Your friend's full of shit." I just wanted a story—any story—that would explain where he'd been for the past thirty-two years. For thirty-two years, Mama's heart ached each day from her first tea in the morning until darkness surrounded her. I wanted a story—a story to replace the other story that I'd memorized down to the scars. *He went out in the morning and sat in a cafe instead of going to the exam. He failed.* As simple as that.

I needed to hear a story that was worthy of her heartache. One with a more complicated plot, and if the twist had to be that Ragi had disappeared behind bars, that would still have been better than the tired, old recital.

5

Ramzi went back on his promise of finding Ragi an apartment even though I'd broken down in tears when I told him that I was on the verge of losing everything if things carried on the way they were. He said he was short on funds because he'd spent so much on the apartment and his daughters' university tuition, so as usual, our aunt's daughter and son got involved, and they moved Ragi into a small, empty apartment in our aunt's old house to give me a break while Ramzi tried to find him a more permanent living situation. Ramzi took the news begrudgingly and, while it took a few months, he did end up renting a small apartment for Ragi in a crowded neighborhood nearby after making me promise that I'd consider taking him back when I'd finished my PhD.

6

My cat was in pain all night, throwing up his insides, so I rushed him to the veterinarian, who told me that one of my neighbors had probably poisoned him. He was a black cat that I called Mallarmé, and he used to cling to me like a baby and would sleep beside me in bed. When Ragi arrived, Mallarmé hid under the bed for days, and I even had to take his food to him there because he wouldn't leave the room. Over time, Ragi managed to reach a detente with Mallarmé, who gave him a wide berth, but he'd scratch and hiss if Ragi came too close. He wasn't a friendly cat, but he never attacked anyone like he did Ragi.

I lay Mallarmé down in my bed that night before leaving the room, but when I went in a bit later, he was gone. I found him staggering in front of the bathroom door—just as my father had done before he died—and then it was over. I cried so hard I thought my heart was going to pop out. I wrapped Mallarmé in one of my robes, not a raggedy sheet, and buried him in the garden beside Meesho. That night, I prayed to God that no matter how He chose to end my life, it not be in that house.

Ragi was angry that I didn't invite him to the thesis defense, but I wasn't able to get over the last fight we'd had before he moved out. Even now when I think back on it, I can feel the same bitterness—bitterness and despair. I can remember the long days I spent in my bedroom after, avoiding getting out of bed so that I wouldn't have to see him. I'd just returned from a very short work trip to Italy, which was like a godsend, and although it had been very grueling, I came back with more money than I'd dreamed of. I bought everything Ragi asked me to get him from the duty-free shop, and I even got him a pack of fancy cigarettes that he'd told me he had his eye on. The gifts astounded him. "I couldn't even get this in Germany! Thank you so much. Didn't you get anything at all for yourself?"

"It's no big deal. I will next time!"

"There's Mama's martyr complex," he said, but I chose to ignore the comment so that our evening wouldn't be ruined. When he asked how the poetry reading went, I told him all about it because it was one of the best readings I'd ever taken part in. He lost interest in my story and started playing on the computer, so I started playing with Mallarmé, but then Ragi called me over to see something. There was a photo of a woman on the screen. "What do you think?"

"She's very pretty."

"That's my girlfriend. She's a world-class artist; she's German. I wanted you to see her so you don't start getting ideas about yourself. You're surrounded by idiots here. They think you're a big deal, but you really aren't. You gotta remember there are world-class people out there, so you don't get delusional," he said laughing.

The facade of the older brother collapsed once and for all that night, and even Ragi was taken aback by my anger. He waved his fist in my face and got up close to me, but I didn't flinch. I just stared him down until he took a step back. "I could hit you right now, but I don't hit women."

The word "women" sent a chill through my body, and I locked myself in my bedroom that night, listening to every sound on the other side of the door until sleep overcame me. When I woke up the following evening, everything seemed clear and conclusive. We were two strangers forced to live under the same roof. Why would I invite him to hear me defend a PhD thesis that he thought was insignificant? I'd made my decision.

7

Ramzi returned to Saudi Arabia, but I promised him that we'd deal with the "issue" of Ragi moving back in during his next trip. I was the only thing left in the house, and I found it a struggle to get from my bedroom to the front door because I was having bouts of high blood pressure after the defense. Two millimeters of mercury had me on bed rest.

I, too, could die. The idea came as a surprise even though it was obvious, and as I contemplated it, lying in bed, alone in the house, I started having trouble breathing, and my heart rate was slightly elevated—perhaps in response to the thought itself—so I took some pills, smooth and cold, to settle me. There was nothing strange about a forty-six-year-old woman dying after a sudden heart attack. I'd stopped pursuing death as I'd done in the past, but in that moment, I couldn't tell if I was trying to die or just escape. Racing, speeding toward that non-place they called suicide. Who was it who said that "Only optimists commit suicide?" And what had made me think when I gave up trying to end my life that I would go on playing the same role forever? The role that had been my destiny since birth, since I'd been given my grandmother's name as she lay dying. I was there in the room with her and Mama. I may even have been listening in as they spoke, poking my head out of the birth canal to catch sight of my grandmother's perishing face. A witness to death.

8

We play our roles until we get so good at them that we stop imagining we can play others. We're satisfied with the crumbs left for us by the leads, who are used to playing a variety of roles and basking in applause. We extras accept our roles and never dream of being the star; we prefer it that way because we've already got our lines memorized and we don't have to bother coming up with a character. We play the same part over and over again until we die and then our peers carry us to the grave in a small procession during which they grieve both for us and for themselves with tears that can't be faked.

9

The landlord turned up one month and informed me that he was planning on selling the building. When I told my neighbor about the conversation that I'd had with Mr. Ahmad—the thousandth time he'd warned us that he was going to sell before changing his mind—she quipped, "Here we go again," but it all happened much more quickly than we could've anticipated. The buyer came over the following day, and we discussed what our share would be, but neither one of us tried to negotiate for more. It was way less than what you'd usually get for giving up an apartment in that area, but my neighbor had already agreed to the offer. Her kids had grown up and got married, and she was all alone in the house, so she wanted to move to somewhere new closer to where they lived.

One sunny morning, the landlord brought over a new rental contract with my name on it—so that there wouldn't be any snags with the sale, he told me—and we proceeded to do something miraculous: we tore up the old one that had my mother's scrawl on it. She'd signed the tenancy over to me a few days before she died so that I'd "feel secure." In all those years, I'd never imagined that it could all end so quickly. "It's what your mother would want," my friends and neighbor told me, but I still felt anxious. Salvation seemed so near. Why would God answer my prayers as though He's just hearing them now?

I threw myself into the task, racing frantically against time before anyone could find out what was happening. My friends helped me go through everything in the house, and I didn't mind letting them read every scrap of paper and look at every photograph. "Do you wanna keep it or should we shred this one, too?" I felt like a criminal, careful not to leave any fingerprints at the scene, and I'd decided that I wouldn't take anything with me, either. I put the old furniture out front for anyone who wanted it. They could reupholster it, but I didn't want to have to be there to see it. Maybe some of their excitement would rub off on it and I'd fail to recognize the old furniture, if they ever had me over.

I tore up all my brothers' photos and letters—"The Eruption of Loathing," I called it—because I wanted to wipe out every trace of them. I didn't want anything to follow me back to my new place and stow away in some crack until it could lay siege to me one night. I took a single photo of my father and several photos of Mama and me together, my good clothes, and my books, and then I handed over the key to the new owner and shut the door behind me for the last time.

10

Didn't someone say that fate could be a good accomplice sometimes? Fate keeps an eye out so that we can run away as far as possible. I kept a photo of Mallarmé, which hangs on the wall of my new house. A little talisman. Mallarmé was the only one who saw Ragi's return for what it was. He understood that the missing brother I'd longed to reunite with wasn't the support I'd been expecting. He was just the last pillar in the old house to crumble. One can never know, but I'm pretty sure that Mallarmé took the robe that I'd wrapped him up in after he died and threw it down at God's feet like any scene-chewer, and declared, "She says she doesn't want to die in that house. Is that not something a God can arrange?"

When I finally received a text message from Ramzi, it didn't upset me because I'd been expecting it. It had been four months since the landlord sold our old building, but that was the first he'd heard about it—"my betrayal"—and he was "in shock." It was like "a nightmare," he said. I knew that he wouldn't confront me himself because he couldn't face a full reckoning, but I also knew that he'd make Ragi do it. Ragi called to ask me what had happened—how could

I have abandoned him? For the first time in my life, I suppressed genuine pity and responded in a harsh tone that sounded strange even to me. Then I hung up and changed my number.

No regrets, no memories, no passing by the old house on my way to visit friends in Heliopolis. It was over. The house wasn't even there anymore, the new owner having demolished it, and a new high-rise stood in its place. I tried to go past there just once, but I got confused and couldn't remember exactly where the house had been. That was my one and only attempt. I knew that I'd never find my way back.

It's been fifteen years, and it finally feels that this is where my life began. In my new house. The time I spent in that other place is so much dust.

11

I left the message unread in the Other folder on Facebook Messenger for two days before I opened it. "Dad has been sick for a while. We thought we should let you know in case you wanted to see him." It was from my youngest niece, whom I hadn't got to see grow up. I called her right away, hoping she'd pick up even though she didn't have my number saved. "Hello. Who's this?"

"It's your aunt. What's wrong with your father?" I think she was stunned that I'd got back to her so quickly, and that was when I realized that Ramzi had asked her to message me. She'd written to the stranger as instructed, but she didn't think anything would come of it. I assumed it was something serious if he was trying to contact me again after giving up years ago.

"That's right, Ma'am, my father's dead. We're just leaving the cemetery now. Our lives belong to God." I ended the call without saying a word.

Had Ramzi wanted to see me during one of his moments of lucidity, just like my mother had when she called for both my brothers? Had they put off contacting me until the very last minute because they didn't want him to forgive me and consider changing his will? Or was it just out of obligation—had someone told them they should let all his "relatives" know? Ramzi's daughters were married and had children of their own, so who knows what was going on? Who knows what conversations took place around his comatose body as he lay dying just as our mother had?

Who are these tears for? For him or for her or for the encroaching horizon closing in on me? I'll be locked away, too, one day. "On an evening just like this one."

12

Not much has changed since Ramzi died four months ago. I cried for two days, but then I stopped, and I didn't go to pay my condolences after the funeral. Rather, I posted an announcement of his death on Facebook, and I was gratified to receive many messages of support from my friends. I also got a spiteful thrill from knowing Ramzi's family could see them. I had thought about going to pay my condolences after that phone call, riding the emotional wave all the way to their front door, but I couldn't bring myself to do it. Who was I going there to console? For months, I heard my niece saying "That's right, Ma'am," over and over in my head, and I spent many nights going through Ramzi's Facebook page, which was suddenly accessible to me now that he was dead, reading about the details of his illness.

My friends—even those closest to me—chose to express their sympathies over the phone. The only person who came to pay their respects in person was my psychiatrist because when she'd called to convey her condolences, I couldn't stop bawling, and she wanted to check in on me.

"Ramzi's dead," I say to myself sometimes, "and you just have to accept it. Death and estrangement are two very different things." Sometimes, it makes me cry to hear myself say it.

13

Not much has changed; my routine is what it was: hours are wasted, but from time to time, I write. There are no longer any battles raging to keep me up at night, but for some reason when I do wake up, I imagine seeing the IV bags that were once my constant preoccupation. We all need battles to live. We need them to follow us around like a shadow. I can no longer bring myself to repeat the threat that was constantly on my lips in those final years. Ramzi and Ra'ifa had bumped into each other on the street, and he told her that he knew my new address. "If he so much as shows his face," I would say, but that taunt is meaningless now. I no longer have to imagine every possible bloody confrontation.

Ramzi never turned up. Not once. Never stood on the other side of the fence like a guilty child. I would have opened the door, but it didn't happen. Another door opened and then it shut behind him forever.

14

I learned from Ahmad Wahby, the old landlord, that Ramzi had abandoned Ragi two years before he died. He and his family had moved from Heliopolis to New Cairo without telling him, and I realized that I'd been his inspiration. He, too, had run away—no regrets, no memories.

Mr. Ahmad also told me that my aunt's sons had moved Ragi, who was in his seventies now, into a nursing home, and the reminder of Ragi's age threw me for a loop. I asked him to get Ragi's address because I thought I might go visit him and maybe even bring him back to live with me. The guilt kept me up all night, but by the following morning, I was having second thoughts. A few days later, I got news that the only link between me and my cousins—that was the story I told myself at least—had died. My connection to my cousins, and thus to Ragi, was severed when our former landlord passed away. I felt a vague grief, which was more than I would have anticipated.

I'm going to have to make an effort to reconnect with my family and find out where Ragi's living. I'd cut contact with all of them when I moved into my new house, even the ones who'd been good to me. They'd expected me to work off my debts, as though I'd been tied to our old house by invisible strings for the past forty years. All they could see when they looked at me was a figure stuck to the wall, like Ragi's pet spider. The spider—naked, desperate, and panicked, its mouth stuffed with flies—had finally made a break for it.

I paused my plan to search for Ragi for the time being and repeated the fortifying mantra of my sixties: Didn't someone say that fate could be a good accomplice sometimes?

Auntie Saadeya, our former nanny, had also passed away. She'd lived into her eighties, far longer than anyone had expected. I kept putting off going to see her for an entire year after I learned she was sick by using work as an excuse, but I printed a small obituary for her in the newspaper. I felt dismal for a while, but I didn't cry.

Three deaths in four months, but no grief or rather only a stillborn grief. It came into the world when Ramzi died but struggled to breathe once or twice before dying itself. I bore witness to the three deaths—as I've always done—each following in even quicker succession, and it felt as though a director was pushing me out onto the stage. I was always an extra so no one had ever bothered to give me any lines. All I can do now is improvise.

Three deaths back to back, as if they're trying to catch up to one another. They want to make it into at least one scene alongside the leading man. Three deaths back to back. They echo in my heart like les trois coups—"Bang . . . bang . . . bang"—just as the curtain is about to rise.

www.ingramcontent.com/pod-product-compliance
Lightning Source LLC
Jackson TN
JSHW080009160425
82711JS00001B/1

* 9 7 8 1 6 4 9 0 3 3 2 0 8 *